Prague Days and Nights

by James Tressler

The English Teachers

When we arrived in Prague, there was a driver to pick up all the new prospective teache at Ruzny Airport. For many of us it was our first time abroad, so we were raw, eager anc lost.

There were teacher training schools all over the city. Ours was located in a small hotel i the Vysocany in Prague's 9th District on the fareast side of the city. It was an industrial area during Communist times, and still is in many respects, but gentrification and grow has led to new, smart office buildings, flats and landscaping.

But when we arrived, this change was still a few years ahead, and since it was winter, t district looked dirty, grey, un-picturesque. Down the steps in the metro station you saw men sitting over pints of beer and shots of *slivovice* at seven in the morning before head off to their construction or factory jobs. At the shop where you went to get cigarettes a d a brown terrier, padded and sniffed down the aisle while its owner worked the cash register. At the street food stands you ordered a fried cheese sandwich (*smazeny syr*) drowned in ketchup and mayonnaise, or else a hamburger that tasted vaguely of balone and was served with cole slaw and cucumbers instead of lettuce and tomato. Then of course were the rows of panalaky, rising like grey monoliths in the distance.

The school was located in a small room adjacent to the hotel. Every month a new crop o eighteen to twenty trainees passed through the school. Considering the prices we paid f the course, we surmised the school must have been making a fair chunk of money. Eng was a booming micro-business in Prague, and in much of Europe, as it would later be further East in places like China and South Korea. Companies wanted their employees t possess a minimum level of English for emails, phone calls, conferences with clients anc affiliates abroad. That's where we came in.

During the four-week course, which was really sort of a boot camp for teachers, we were immersed in teaching – live teaching – every day. In fact, the first day we arrived, we'd hardly set our bags down and gone through a course overview when the very next day w were teaching Czech students. The students were given a discount, much like when you have your hair cut at a barber college.

Our trainers, Paul and Terry, were excellent and were experienced and qualified teacher who had taught all over the world before deciding to open a school together in Prague. T team-taught us, with Paul usually taking the first half of the morning and Terry the second. Paul would, for example, give us a lesson in basic Czech, greetings and introductions, and afterward he would break down the lesson, show us how we had managed to learn this basic Czech without having used any English to understand it. H method was proven, effective, and it was from Paul's lessons that we learned the invalua technique of modelling, eliciting, suggestion; teaching to a large degree resembles acting showing rather than merely telling. Such techniques I found later on to be crucial when working with beginners. With higher-level students you could depend less on modelling

:e by then they had acquired enough language to understand and communicate. But ı lower levels you had to model a lot.

m Terry, we learned the value of sneaking up on the students, misdirection: make them ık they are learning one thing when in fact you're teaching them another, that way y're more relaxed and not over-focused. This was especially true with grammar lessons. ɔu tell a student, let's study grammar, you'll see a lot of eyes frost over, Terry explained. tead, Terry showed us a bunch of photographs.

is is my sister," he said, pointing to a young woman in a bikini sitting on a beach and ling. "Do you know where she is?"

guessed a few places.

hiti," Terry said. "She was there last year. When was she there?"

st year," we said.

ng to the board, Terry drew a time line indicating "past," "present" and "future." Then ving his pen, he arrived at the "future" point on the timeline.

re?" he asked.

we said.

ry scratched his head, theatrically puzzled.

re?" he pointed at the "present."

again.

, yes. Here." He arrived at the "past" and we nodded in agreement. Terry made a point scratching his head. "Is she there now?" he asked.

we said.

at's right," Terry said. "She's not there now." And he wrote the sentence on the board. sister was in Tahiti last year," and then underlined the words "was" and "last year," d drew an arrow connecting them. "The action is finished," Terry continued, making a pping motion with his hand. "Finished."

d so we had "learned" past simple. I realize for other teachers reading this my rendering Terry's method is a bit simplistic; they'll notice a few details missing. But I just wanted give a sense of how he taught, not go into a grammar lesson. It's hard for me to capture ry's energetic, lively personality, the jokes he told. He was breezy, almost glib, as though nuts and bolts of the language were merely an afterthought.

told us of past trainees and their problems, such as the trainee who spoke eight erent languages.

's teaching a group of elementary students," Terry said. "And he's trying to teach them word 'superfluous.' Superfluous! As if that's a useful word for an elementary level dent! Anyway, he brought in this stuffed toy shark and he shows it to the students, and s like this – 'superfluous!' And he tosses the shark across the room and lands with this thud. You see the students eyes following the shark as it flies through the air. The cher kept going over and picking up the toy shark and kept repeating: 'Superfluous!' Do ı get it? *Superfluous!*" and he'd toss the shark across the room again, the students eyes ɔt watching this shark fly across the room and you could see they thought he was nuts! erward, we all joked about him: speaker of eight languages, master of none."

got a good laugh, and there were many other stories. They all had a point, just like the ɔerfluous stuffed grey shark. We listened and I think we all quietly dreaded being the t of one of these funny stories to future trainees. We imagined them shaking their heads d laughing at us too, so we tried to absorb the moral of each story as much as we ghed.

er the morning lessons with Paul and Terry, we would be split into groups of three and signed a class to teach. The teachers in each group would teach the class for forty five nutes, rotating, with two evaluating the teacher who was in front of the class. We also d informal evaluations by Paul or Terry each day. To pass the course we would go ough two formal observations.

e key point we learned and were constantly reminded about was the importance of son plans, of having a clear objective going in and a step-by-step plan for how the students would reach that goal. For example: Today the students will demonstrate the ability to talk about future plans and intentions, using 'going to' and 'will,' and outline course material, exercises and activities.

The language schools and companies that recruited teachers in Prague periodically sent feedback, and we were told one of the most common complaints regarding teachers was their lack of preparation. Terry and Paul were going to make damn sure we didn't leave t course not knowing how to prepare a lesson plan. They drilled it into us, as a matter of fact.

And they emphasized the importance of sticking to the plan (later we of course found tha in companies for various reasons this wasn't always possible).

Once, while Terry was observing one of my lessons with a group of pre-intermediate students, he noticed me stumble, lose my place and was unsure where I was supposed t go next. I recovered, but as soon as the lesson ended, and the students were saying goodbye and filing out, Terry was sitting there looking at me with this head-shaking, bemused grin.

"Lose your lesson plan?" he asked. Terry was from Birmingham in England and had a direct, Midlands style of speaking. I was aware of my error, but didn't know what to say.

"You were fumbling and farting around up there! You thought you could just go up there and wing it, didn't you? A word of advice: stay with your lesson plan. Keep it somewhere you can refer to it."

Another time, with an elementary level class, I handed out a text for the students to reac

"In five minutes," I instructed, "you'll have read the text and we can discuss it."

The students just looked at me. I froze. "Read," I said, pointing to the text. That worked a they started reading.

"'You'll have read? 'You will have read?'" Terry asked pointedly after the lesson. "That's future perfect tense. They won't learn that for another three years, you moppet!. So when you said that you lost them. But then you saw that your modelling saved you. You point at the text and just said, 'Read the text.' That was perfect. Remember to grade your language for the level. Keep your instructions clear and simple."

That was Terry's style of mentoring: tough, no-nonsense, with a bit of English piss-takin thrown in.

Paul, by contrast, was low key, "professional" in his assessments. In a relaxed, level voic he'd point out the things in your lesson he'd liked, then go over a few points you still needed to work on. In that sense Paul played good cop and Terry bad cop. I think they di this deliberately, maybe even rehearsed it beforehand. It was an act, but at the same tim valid, proven and effective approach.

You sensed they knew where we needed to go, and had faith in their assessments. That way you weren't offended or hurt, especially if they called you out right in front of everybody. Like I said, it was kind of a boot camp, intensive, each day packed from start finish with activities, and you felt yourself slowly transforming into the makings of a teacher. Paul and Terry were the two tested veterans who were preparing us for the realit of the battlefield, the classroom, the companies.

"Some of these teachers," Terry told us. "They go to work for a school, and a week later they're emailing me complaining that they have to get up at six in the morning, get a bus across town to teach in company, or that they have to work at nine in the evening." He looked at us and shook his head. "They come over here to Prague from England or Ameri and they think they're on holiday. And as soon as they find out that they have to work, t it's no different from anywhere else, they run home to mum and dad and the Thanksgivi turkey!"

. Lights

ıe evenings we all often went together for meals. There were several places in the ;hbourhood, but the closest one was Café Lyra. I stopped by there a couple of years c and it's been bought by a new owner and completely renovated. Back then it was a modest place, warmly lit in the evenings, and the walls were covered with paintings by :h artists. The food was a little bit over-priced, but it was decent Czech fare – pork, ash, other meat dishes served with the inevitable dumplings (*knedliky*), sourkraut or cabbage and chopped carrots passing for a salad, and of course several pints of beer. said, we all usually went out together and when we arrived, a big group, some of the ls would look at us and the waiters would find room at a couple tables and we'd sit ther and talk about the day, about ourselves and where we came from, about Prague, ıt other capitals – Vienna, London, Paris – and you suddenly realized how close they e now. It was an exciting time. Here, you thought, was Europe; here was travel and ting people; here, was the world. You were in this interesting new course, learning to be acher, and fulfilling a lifelong dream: Europe, the very heart of it, and soon you would eeing all of it.

ıe of the teachers were already quite seasoned. There was Warren and his girlfriend, y, for instance, who had travelled extensively across the Continent; there was Adam his girlfriend, who sang opera, and after the course they were planning to move to in where she could try and break into the theatre. Some of the people who had already elled around could be a bit aloof, you could tell they looked upon you as someone fresh ı America. In those days with the wars in Iraq and Afghanistan really heating up, along ı anti-Americanism in Europe, to be a fresh American wasn't exactly fashionable.

as Martin and Paul who I came to be close to. Most days we sat together and, when sible, taught together and in the evenings, went to Lyra for dinner, relaxing in its warm, -lit atmosphere. Paul was a Scotsman in his thirties then, about my age, and was ried to a Russian woman. They lived in London, but Paul had come over to Prague for course. He had a really deep, resonant Scottish accent and he was literary like I was so :ould always discuss authors and books, as well as our own hopes to write, and he was ays sympathetic and helpful.

tin was the wild card in our group. He was only about twenty one then but he's one of e guys who at that age everybody thought was older. He acted older, had a savvy ıkle in his Irish eyes, that drew people to him and listen to what he had to say. was born in Rathmullen, which I was later to visit and found to be a lovely, isolated side town in the northernmost tip of Ireland. The region is known as Donegal. I ember telling this to Orla, a teacher who was from Wexford. She was impressed, as t Irish tend to be.

"They're all on their own 'p there," she said, with a long, impressive sigh. And I rememb listening to her, this was one evening in Reigrove Sady, imagining Donegal as this lonel haunted place on the ragged edge of the earth, the image of the people too, desperate ar reaching heavenward to be delivered, and, having failed that, had resigned to a tough, romantic and embattled existence. As I said, later on when, at Martin's invitation I visit staying at his parents' house, I found that image to be far from the truth. Donegal, and town of Rathmullen, are lovely and isolated, but no more so than the little northern California towns I'd known for many years.

Martin had worked for a bar in Donegal and when he came over to Prague, had manage secure unemployment payments. So he was living on the dole: each Friday his bank account was topped up via electronic deposit. We all heard about it and we envied Mart and wished we had been clever enough to manage that. It meant that, unlike a lot of us Martin didn't have to scramble and worry about finding work at one of the schools as sc as the course ended. By then, my own savings brought from America were already getti low (it didn't help that of course we were out every night), and I worried more than most think.

"It's not easy," Martin would say, when he saw me worrying.

"It's not," I'd say. That became our sort of saying: "It's not easy." "No, it's not."

Funnily enough the first night I met Martin I didn't like him. The class had gone on a to of Prague. This guy Jose, from Las Vegas, who'd finished in one of the courses ahead of acted the expert. He took delight in showing us how to buy a metro ticket, all big smiles and jokes that he thought were tremendously funny. We all went with him onto the met and got out at Mustek and walked to Old Town Square, then down past the Starometsk metro station, across the Manesova Bridge to Mala Strana. Jose showed us the peeing statues at the Kafka Museum, and soon we were crossing the Charles Bridge and back to Old Town. All this time I walked with Paul and we walked behind all the others, just taking in the sights ourselves. It was my first time really seeing it, and it was exciting ar wanted to see it for myself and not have somebody like Jose ruining it with his tourist s

After the tour we all sojourned to what we called the Dutch Bar, just off Dlouha Street n Bohemia Bagel. It was called that because the owner then, Casper, was Dutch. He looke little like pictures of Van Gogh, and was very laid-back. Years later we heard that he'd developed multiple schlerosis and was confined to a wheel chair, the bar sold, and we a felt bad – Casper was a really good guy.

We all were excited after the walk and we ordered big cheeseburgers and potatoes and b pints of beer. It got late and we drank, each taking turns ordering rounds (it was that da met Chris, Mad Chris, his hair shooting high up from his forehead). Anyway it got later the talk had gone round and somehow had shifted to the war.

"Yeah, you guys are getting' yer asses kecked over there," this voice next to me said. It w Martin, and I remember I was drunk then, everybody was, and I remember thinking he intrusive, arrogant. But then a couple nights later we all went out and he turned out to really cool, and we became friends. I told him I didn't like him when we first met and Martin thought it was funny, and even told it to Paul and other people. He told us too th during the tour, Jose, the tour guide had come up to Martin at a party the night before.

"I'm Jose!" he had said, flashing his tour guide grin.

"I don't care," Martin had said.

That's when I knew we were going to be good friends.

Sex Tourists

re was a distinct feeling, for me, that the Prague I was seeing upon my arrival that first ter was the last of an old phase, the phase that had begun with the 1989 revolution. Czechs had joined the EU that year, and not long after that the visa restrictions, ays a huge gray area, began to get tighter. Also, later on there began to be talk of a king ban in the pubs, as had already happened in Paris and London . Things that le Prague the New Wild East in the Nineties, the nightclubs, the relaxed attitudes to king and drugs and sex, the corruption in the public sector, and the wide open stment opportunities for prescient Westerners, were beginning to wane by the time I ved, though they were still around. "Prague seems to be losing its old alcoholic charm," te one disappointed expat on one of the websites, a statement that seemed to sum up t I wrote of the city seemingly on the verge of a new phase.

king back, I think the impression I had at that time was marred, or blurred. I think t I really meant was that the edgy Prague of the Nineties was gone. I was experiencing sunset of that time, when to be an American or Englishman in the former Eastern bloc seen as something hip. By the time I arrived, we were at the point of becoming passé. iliarity breeds contempt. Plus, the anti-American sentiment that was beginning to get nger throughout Europe, in the wake of the war, was also beginning to be felt in Prague at's not to suggest Americans were badly treated, far from it. I think, looking back, the eymoon was over, that's all. Czechs were learning to view Americans with a bit more achment, circumspection. During the Cold War the socialists' propaganda dictated the st was corrupt, decadent. This view gave way to an almost child-like admiration after the olution. It was inevitable, healthy, that these extreme viewpoints stand back for a more anced view.

long after my arrival I had dinner with the night news editor from Radio Free Europe, was an old colleague of my city editor in America . He chose the place, an expensive rist restaurant on Old Town Square.

r a dinner of roasted pork neck and mashed potatoes, washed down with pints of ner-Urquell and a digestive, we talked about Prague .

not like it was before," my companion conceded. "Back in those days the place was zy. You felt Paris in the Twenties must have been something like this. But nowadays, it's an average, Central European capital. The show's moved on ... East is the way to go, ng man! Have you thought about Budapest? Even Shanghai ... that place is bustling se days. Go East, young man!"

ny do you stay in Prague?" I asked.

shrugged.

on't know. I'm too old, I guess. In most places the food's bad, overpriced, the people are e. Oh, wait, I do know! It's Prague! And the women! It's the women who keep me here. I must have now, what? Three girlfriends? Whew! God bless 'em! They haven't changed sc much, thank God."

It was over dinner that evening, listening to the news editor from Radio Free Europe talk about Prague and the old days, that I had that impression that I was arriving just at the sunset of a special time. It was this Prague you saw in photos hanging on the walls in places the Chateau.

We also talked about news and about writing, and he encouraged me to stay away from politics – nobody knew or cared about them – and to write about the pubs and the night life, the slices of little Bohemia. "I know! Why don't you do a survey of the brothels?" he suggested at one point. "You could probably sell that back somewhere in America."

It was good advice, but as it turned out later, it's very difficult to write about these thing when you are caught up in them, as I was. Plus, coming from a small town, I was for a l time too impressed and wide-eyed to be able to make much sense of my new surroundir and to put them in any kind of perspective. It was much more fun to just get lost in it al tantalizing series of charming streets, a maze of bars and nightclubs, to follow the trail c cigarette smoke, to spin beneath the hazy strobe lights, the beats of the discos, the dangerous beauty in the Slavic eyes of the girls at Paradise or Atlas or Darling.

Back in our first winter in Prague , we didn't know the city very well. Some of us knew it little better than others, knew which night tram to take at Wenceslas Square to back ba across the river after midnight after the metro had closed.

We were all new to Prague after dark, and although most of us were far from naïve, we fe like freshmen at their first party. I was older than most of the others and should have known better, but in those days I'd just left America having spent a decade in a very sma town in Northern California . In those days, I had a very neat and clever philosophy: you spent the past ten years making good decisions, so you owe it to yourself to make a few ones. I made no secret of this philosophy, which I was very proud of, and found in Pragu great many people willing and ready to support me on it.

Martin was the first, and he introduced me to Terry, and to Larkin and Steve and Paul, a of course Charlie. There were others but this was the core original group. All of us arrive in Prague about the same time, did the same teaching training course, except for Charlie and Larkin, who went to different schools.

In the evenings, we would start at Marquis de Sade, a wonderful pub in Old Town not fa from the Tyn Church . The Marquis is long gone now. But in those days it was the perfe warm-up meeting place. Afterward, we would migrate a block down to the Chapeau, or Chateau as it was called then. Downstairs at Chateau was where you could score ecstas Upstairs some Algerian guys sold cocaine and marijuana and stronger stuff in the men's toilet. Usually we stuck to ecstasy, at about 250 crowns per pill, and then we walked through the dark, snowy streets into New Town and to Nebe. Between the beer and the ecstasy pills, which just began to kick in during the ten minute walk, we would be trollie by the time we arrived at Nebe. Then in a kind of warp several hours would pass, and we found ourselves usually at Le Clan and it would be three or four in the morning.

At Le Clan we sat with Russians (I think this is where we met Pavel, the drug dealer who became good friends and partners with Martin and Charlie) and did lines of coke to wake up and then at six grabbed a taxi or just walk down near the main train station to Studi 54, not that we really knew where we were going in those days.

We would stay out most evenings until daybreak when, broke, shattered, cold, we'd find the metro open and the people on it were heading to work, and we would go home and crash. We'd wake up late in the afternoon, one of us went down the hill to the potraviny and came back with the cheap rolls called rohliky, as well as eggs, cheese and we would have a numb, meager breakfast, all completely drained, zombie-like. Then we might go back to sleep for a couple hours or watch a film, then head out for dinner and the evenir would start all over again. As you can imagine, not much writing ever got done.

Martin was the leader, if we even had one. He was a young tough-gentle Irishman from Donegal. I say he was the leader because of all of us, people took a shine to him, and ays wanted to know where he was going. Also, Martin had a cheerful, leering talent for ing us into places and situations that we could never have managed without him. He Terry were both that way. It was they who led us into places like Le Clan and Studio; had a knack those two for picking up people and finding places to get into trouble. So always had what we needed, especially in the way of the many forms of madness.

rlie was the youngest, he was only nineteen then, and had interrupted his studies at to come over to Prague . When he came to look at the flat his mom was with him, and thought for a moment he might be really square, but he turned out to be ready for thing. Paul, a Scotsman, was closer to my age, and had a master's degree in English ature. On many hungover mornings at the flat we would sit, just the two of us, and uss Hemingway or Thomas Hardy or Dostoevsky. Paul had a wife in London , but they traveled a lot, as some married couples do.

tin showed us the Paradise Club. One night it was after four, the Metro was closed, and didn't feel like waiting around for the night tram. It was really cold out and Old Town nearly deserted. Martin said he knew a place where we could shake off the cold and some time until the metro opened. I know I didn't care where we were going, as long as as somewhere warm.

en we arrived, the doorman seemed to know Martin (doormen always knew Martin), and gave us a reduced cover charge, then searched us and then we went in. Techno music pulsating and the interior was soft lit. A girl was dancing up on the stage. We looked t the girl and into the room. A whole bevy of young women were sitting at the tables, all of them turned and fixed an eye on*you*, and smiled invitingly. There is nothing quite that: coming off a cold street at four a.m. and walking into a room full of enticing ng women, all of them looking at you as if they have been expecting you.

esteem of Martin, already high, rose even further. This was a guy who really knew ere to go at four in the morning on a cold night. We found a table and sat down, it was rtin, Paul and I, and within ten seconds we each had a girl sitting with us, all of them ndly and good-looking. You immediately forgot all about being cold or tired and the ning seemed to be starting all over again.

girl's name was Kristina, or so she said. She was a very pretty, busty brunette with id blue eyes and a bright summer dress gave her full figure lots of attention. She spoke y gently in English, stroking my face, inviting me to touch her. She asked lots of things, where I was from, what I was doing in Prague , and she asked if I wanted to buy her a nk. I did and immediately saw my error. The bill came and the drink, a screwdriver, was) crowns, which then was nearly 30 dollars. Martin and Paul laughed about it, me ing for such an easy scam, but in a way I didn't care. Kristina was sweeter than ever, l, sipping the screwdriver through a straw, asked if I wanted to go upstairs. "Do you like body?" she asked. "If you come upstairs you can see all of it, you can touch me where you want."

we went upstairs. I had to pay first, and we worked out the price, it came to about 2,000 wns, if I remember, and we went up a dark, winding stairwell.

club closed sometime after six, and it was still dark outside when we left. Kristina had nged into street clothes and actually was quite friendly. She let me put a kiss on her ek and she smiled and bid us good night and went to find her car and the rest of us nt to get the metro.

er the next couple days, I thought about Kristina a lot, how nice she had been. I told self she really had a heart of gold, and was only working at a place like the Paradise b by chance. She had given me her number and over the next day or two I sent ssages asking her if she would like to meet and have dinner. She always responded with of x's and o's. She wanted to meet me, but I had to come down to the club and see her. guys laughed and I saw they were right, and I wasn't upset. There was nothing to be set about.

e night we hit Marquis briefly, then wound down to Nebe, where we ingested the last of ecstasy pills.

"Nebe is the perfect mid-evening club," Charlie reflected. "What's that?" I asked. "You start at Marquis for the early going. Then Nebe, from 11 to, say, four. Then it's La Clan, then Studio for the wrap." That's pretty much the route the evening followed, except at Paul's urgent request we substitute La Clan for the Paradise Club. The Paradise Club is strip bar-brothel just off the main square. Every time Barnie was in town he made it a point to stop by. The sex clubs then were full every weekend with young and not-so-you men taking advantage of cheap flights from London to Prague, and the legendary stories how cheap and easy the sex was and how beautiful Prague women are. Most of the abov true, though most of the women, although good-looking, are mostly Ukrainian and Russ working in the clubs while their boyfriends or husbands sit at home. When we got there must have been about four-thirty. A "live sex show" was in progress on the main stage a the club was full. The girls were either sitting up at the bar waiting for you to buy them drink or working the tables. Most of them were in a bad mood and wanted to hurry you because it was late and they were tired, or they had taken something and were blissfully blank-eyed happy. We were sitting at Paradise for about an hour. Several women sat wit us, Martin and Paul rose, taking two of them by the hand. "We're going upstairs," Martir yelled over the music. "You guys watch our coats." He meant Charlie and I, and Terry, a American teacher who at that moment was engaged in an intense argument with some o the girls. Charlie got up to use the toilet, so for a few minutes I sat by myself.

Presently I looked up. A tall, elegant looking young woman in a bright blue evening dres was walking to the table.

"Hello," she said. "You know this isn't just a bar."

"I know," I said.

"You would like to go upstairs?"

The ectasy had long since worn off, and I was tired. It was nice just to look at her; I had that sudden awful loneliness that comes with clarity after a night of partying.

"So you want to go?" she asked, a little startled.

I said yes, so she took my hand and led me to a cash register at the bar. Then we went u circular staircase, at the top of which was a dark corridor. A short line of people stood, apparently waiting for rooms. I passed Martin and Paul, who were with their girls. We all laughed and waved hysterically to each other, as if we were a couple housewives runnin into each other at the supermarket on a Sunday afternoon. "What's your name?" I asked the girl. "Olga," she said. Olga must have had some pull, because she marched us past t line. An old woman handed her a plastic bag, which Olga then passed to me. Inside was towel, some soap and a condom. She then beckoned me to follow her to a back room. Th room was much bigger and more impressive-looking than I would have imagined. A king- sized bed, with freshly pressed sheets, sat in the middle of the room, and light club musi played softly from unseen speakers. "So first – shower," Olga said. I guessed she meant r I went into the bathroom and quickly undressed. The water was piping hot, it felt good a a long night at the bars. She'd just finished taking her clothes off and was laying the dre neatly over a chair near the bed. She had adopted a cold professional attitude. After a couple minutes, I rolled over and looked at the ceiling. "What's the matter?" Olga got up. Now she looked a little nervous or worried. I think she was worried I might complain to t management. "Nothing."

"Is there something I could do for you? I'm sorry, it's just, I work here five years. I don't want to do this anymore."

"Where are you from?" I asked.

"Here. Czech."

"Are you a student?"

"Yes."

"What do you study?"

"Art and photography. And you? You are British?"

"American." "American? And you are on holiday?"

"No, teaching."

ching – what?"

glish."

glish, of course." She sighed. "Another English teacher."

she was more conciliatory now, stroking my cheek.

know, I meet a lot of Americans here. Most of them are quite arrogant. But you – you not like them. You talk to me like I am a real person. You want my advice? Don't come ."

made a gesture around the room. "And don't look! The right one, she will come."

n the time was up I went into the bathroom, showered quickly again and got dressed. was already dressed when I came out, and her manner had shifted back to formality. went downstairs, and she disappeared into the crowd with a friendly little wave.

rlie and Terry were sitting at the table.

v was it?" they both said, big grins on their faces.

at," I lied.

rlie was laughing. "You should have seen it. They almost threw Terry out. All the girls sed to go upstairs with him."

k off!" Terry said. "That's not what happened at all! That's not it. I'll tell you later."

kept an eye on the stairs and presently Martin and Paul came down. Then one of the , the one who'd been with Paul came rushing up behind. She said something to him he blew her a kiss, waved and she went back upstairs.

Prague nights!" Paul said, returning to the table.

Breakfast at Studio

We had a flat in Dejvice, one of the most elegant neighbourhoods in Prague. There are wonderful examples of art deco, 1920s houses, and the streets are all tree-lined, well-ke and pleasant. Our place was at the top of a hill at the the Hadkova tram stop. The flat w spacious, with a balcony and lovely view of Prague castle and all the way to the Zizkov tower. The flat had belonged to an old Czech woman, but when she died she left it to he family, and they rented it to pay for their son's education. The son's name was Dave, an he'd spent some time in America, so he spoke really good English and and had acquirec kind of veneer of American gestures and sayings.
"I know, guys," he'd say whenever he came over and saw the place was a mess, beer bot and ashtrays full of cigarette butts, and the toilet so filthy it was "absolutely *nuclear*," a: Martin said. "OK, I know. I *know*! Prague is cool, the clubs are cool, the beer is cheap, t women nice. But come on guys! This is my grandmother's flat! See those windows?" He pointed to the windows with the Prague view. "Those windows cost 10,000 crowns. Plea: guys, I know, I know you like to party, but please clean the place (It looks terrible!) and please, whatever you do, please, please don't break the windows."
We tried to be careful. Once a week or so we'd run the vacuum, and we washed the dish and took the beer bottles down to the *potraviny*, where you could recycle them and they paid you enough that you could actually get more beer. Every now and then Dave's mot who didn't speak any English, would come over and she and Dave would give the place good, solid cleaning. They'd use acid to clean the toilet and shower.
Meanwhile, we met women and brought them to the flat. We dubbed the flat the "bunny ranch," this after one night all three of us came home with women we'd picked up from bars. It was a lot of fun for a while, a long while, while it lasted.
One night I came home and for some reason, kicked the glass in on the door downstairs and then went up to bed. It was one of many irrational things ("You owe it to yourself to make a few bad decisions") that later on you cannot explain to anyone except to say, you were out all night. I thought with that kind of logic that know one would be able to gues who did it.
Of course, a few hours later I was shaken awake. It was Dave, the young guy whose parents owned the flat. He said he knew it was I who had broken the glass. The old wom who lived on the first floor had heard the noise when I came in and so she knew it was c of us who lived upstairs.
"She told me everything," Dave went on. "She says you all are always drinking, singing, fucking girls, coming home late!"
All of this was true, but in that moment of guilt about the window – I was horrified wher woke up and saw the look on Dave's face and remembered – it all sounded like unimaginable horrors. Martin and Charlie had been out late too and they were sleeping when Dave came knocking loudly at the door. One of Charlie's UCLA buddies was in tow that weekend and it was he who answered the door. Dave came in. "Tell him I'm not her Martin called sleepily from the bed, but it was too late. Martin told me all this later. He s Dave came in and immediately accused Martin of breaking the door. "I know it was you! he said, pointing at Martin, who was naked and sprawled out on the bed. Dave was

vinced that Martin was some kind of ringleader of foreign louts, a troublemaker, and were his cohorts.

tin denied breaking the door, though he told me he had seen it when he and Charlie e in, and that's when Dave came in to roust me out of bed. The damage was 1,000 wns, he told me. I didn't have the money, and Martin only had a few hundred, but rlie pitched in, and so did his UCLA buddy. Dave calmed down a lot after he got the ney. He even laughed a little. He told us how the old lady downstairs was all worked up how she hated us, how she was convinced we were a pack of foreign devils and he nt to throw us out. "I had to buy her chocolates to calm her!" he told us.

r that, Dave had a long talk with us, and we promised there would be no more dents (this was after the time the washing machine broke and his mother and the nber had found a condom blocking the pipe. "I don't know," Dave had said, when that pened, protesting that he didn't want to know. "I don't know! Maybe somebody is cing somebody on the washing machine.")

could tell he liked us, as Martin pointed out that morning after Dave left. He kind of ed us for what he imagined as all the wild, sex-filled nights we were having. We did e sometimes, but he imagined us having even wilder and crazier times than we actually The part about the condom in the washing machine, that had affected him, you could him imagining one of us banging a girl on the washing machine. He imagined doing it self, and probably wondered which girl would be the best one to try it with. He gined us screwing in the kitchen, on his grandmother's sofa, on the balcony, even up he roof.

ne had a kind of cock-eyed admiration for us, though he of course had to side with the woman and his parents.

could also say the same about the next-door neighbours. They were a young couple a two young children. They imagined us living in all kinds of sin and debauchery. The was young, slender and very pretty. She had a soft spot for us, you could tell, and ays averted her eyes shyly and smiled in an embarrassed, indulgent way whenever we her. She just asked us, with a note on the door in polite English, not to throw our rette butts off the balcony because her children were very young and played in the d. Her little boy was very sweet and whenever you saw him he always said, "Dobry den!" ne formal, sing-songy Czech style. When the other neighbors wanted something they called out "Hey, English!"

time I came home in the morning from the center without my key and the guys were out. I knocked on the next door neighbor's door. It was Sunday morning and you could they were having a nice quiet lunch. The husband didn't look up from his plate, and children were all saying, "Dobry den!" and the wife, shy and embarrassed as always, erstood the situation and let me walk out to their balcony and cross over to ours. But balcony was locked too so I just lay down on the balcony and slept in the sun until tin and Charlie came home several hours later. "What the fuck are you doing out on balcony?" Martin asked, when he got home.

morning Martin came home and he said Charlie was still at Studio. He had met up a some Swiss guy on holiday and they had spent all night out popping pills and aking with this large group of people. When Martin and I woke up in the afternoon rlie still hadn't come home, and we started to worry. Martin tried calling Charlie on his bile and got no response. So he decided to go back to Studio and try to find him and ng him home. "Christ, he's probably *dead*," Martin said, in grim Donegal humor, putting his jacket and heading out. I stayed at the flat in case Charlie came in while Martin was

er Martin called and said he had found Charlie outside Studio. He was all dirty and neveled, like he had fallen into the grass or bushes, and he appeared not to know where was or even who he was. The thing that really impressed Martin, scared him, when he Charlie was not this, however:

vas his *head*," he told me over the phone. "His head was huge!"

Martin and I worried that it could be some kind of brain damage from too many pills,an
we thought about the prospect of having to call his parents in California. Fortunately, b
the time Martin got Charlie back to the flat, he seemed relatively normal. The swelling o
whatever there had been had gone down, and he seemed coherent, just tired. Dave
happened to be passing by and Martin said he took one look at Charlie and laughed anc
made a drinking pantomime. "Crazy!" he said, and patted Charlie on the back. Charlie
went to bed and slept all that Sunday. In the morning he was fine.

Then there was the time when Martin gave his keys to Pavel, the Russian drug dealer whom they did business with at the clubs. Pavel, Martin told me later, had some girl he wanted to bang but he didn't have anywhere to take her. He couldn't take her to his flat because his girlfriend was there. They had already taken some ecstasy and Martin, feeli that mad "love" the ecstasy produces, magnanimously drew his keys from his pocket an offered them to Pavel. I was out with some other people that night and didn't know anything about it.

When I got home and started to unlock the door it was suddenly opened by this guy I recognized as Pavel, the Russian drug dealer. He was standing there in the foyer buck nakedand holding a mobile phone. Behind him this pretty blonde girl was naked under Martin's sheet and she smiled politely. "Tell Martin everything is cool," Pavel said, handi me the phone.

"Everything's cool," I said.

"Tell him not to steal anything!" Martin's voice was far away, lost in the club sounds, an he kept saying it over and over again. "Tell him not to steal anything!"

For the record, nothing was stolen, and that particular night was put away.

Anyway all those nights were very wild and destructive, and we always woke up very lat the afternoon, feeling depressed with the loss of serotonin, and the long hours. The thin was Studio, as Martin so often reminded us, *didn't even open* until six a.m. and it staye open well into the afternoon. Terry once stayed until five in the afternoon. We always sa would be better just once, to go to bed at a reasonable hour, set our alarms, and get up early and go to Studio when it opened. Wouldn't it be different, we reasoned, to show up rested and fresh, *sober*? Instead of going there all trollied and hammered from the all ni party? We reasoned that me might even stand a better chance of meeting women becaus our freshness and sobriety would make us stand out more and we would look and feel better and be capable of coherent conversation.

Breakfast at Studio: was how we christened this fancy notion.

Studio – I don't know how it is now – then was the great after-hours club in Prague. It w where all the night people – dancers, barmen, waiters, prostitutes – went to wind down after their long nights entertaining other people. They had entertained others and now w ready, with almost sullen eagerness, to be entertained themselves.

The women were very beautiful and very hard, their eyes invisible behind pairs of shade even in the dark atmosphere of the club, their expressions both sensual and cruel, orien in their lack of expression. They could be mean as hell if you touched them (Charlie fou that out, he got smacked by a particularly sullen Ukrainian beauty just for inching his a around her during a dance. One look usually told you not to even bother with them. They went their to listen to the DJs, draw a few lines, and forget.

There were many DJs, and the great club song that year, I can still hear it reverberating my ears this very minute, was "So Many Times." It was the great after-hours song of Studio, and when you heard it you knew the best part of the evening (or whatever time i was) was on hand:

So many times, I looked at you
And then I fell in love with you
So many times ... so many times ...

heard these lines sung sweetly and seductively over the synchopated rhythms that e inviting, tantalizing you to step forward onto the dance floor, to draw closer to the ıt. You usually heard the song in those wan, late hours, your mind warbling with :asy and sleep deprivation, and when you heard it you felt this great communion with hese strange night people, even the women, the mean dancers, were smiling now, ing achieved a blissful forgetfulness, and were whirling about. The dance floor was full and the loneliness of the late hour you forgot. The voice rose, becoming plaintative :

nany times, l looked at you
l how l fell in love with you
nany times … so many times …

the crowd was ready for it, and when the great rhythm swelled, kicking into the groove enzy of applause and roars and whistles rose with it, like greeting Lady Night herself ving across the threshold. The sex girls in their dark shades swayed their bodies under blue lights, some of them laughing, some still sullen but rhythmically sullen now, and watched them and listened to that voice "So many times ...) and forgot everything else. forgot that it was by now nearly noon outside, and that perhaps they'd already played same song three hours ago. You didn't notice. It seemed like perpetual midnight there Studio. Outside didn't exist at all.

xisted again the moment you stepped outside, then daylight fell on you like a dazzling, iron curtain, and you felt a little lost and spooky, heading for the metro or to catch the tram back to Dejvice. All the other people on the tram were busy going about their urday or Sunday afternoon while we sat like shell-shocked ghosts, with the night's anity still in our eyes.

never made it down in the morning for the Breakfast at Studio vision like we wanted, we always talked about it.

Anna

It was in this blue-lit, ragged universe that I met Anna. A tall, ravishing girl with fair ski and full lips and deep, mad blue eyes that looked like those of a chained angel. We were at Marquis de Sade that evening, and outside it was winter. Marquis was always warm, pictures of its days as an old bordello hung on the walls, bringing a 19th Century decad charm into the tavern.

Martin, Charlie and I (and Larkin too, he was there) were sitting on a sofa they had on th lower level near the bar. A musician named Spider was up on stage doing Beatles covers and songs like "Beautiful Girl" by INXS. This little guy from Fiji had attached himself to Martin (people had a way of attaching themselves to Martin; they would say, "You're fror Ireland? Oh, my grandmother is Irish!" "So's mine," would be Martin's dry reply.) Anywa this little Fiji guy was on Martin's elbow and in his ear chattering away in high-pitched, broken English and when he wasn't doing that he was trying to sing along with Spider ir words he could hardly understand.

"He's driving me fuckin' *mental!*" Martin said, looking at us desperately.

We all laughed and teased the Fiji guy a little, but he just smiled his bright smile and thought we were encouraging him, so he talked even more and sang louder, and Martin covered his ears with both hands and groaned. "Get away from me, you *monkey*!" Martin could be blunt, even rude, but the musical sound of his Donegal accent somehow took t edge off, made it all right in some weird way.

It was while all this was going on that I noticed up at the bar a girl sitting there. She was sipping a pint of beer and when I looked at her she kind of turned and smiled, so I went to where she was sitting and ordered a beer. I asked, by way of an introduction, if she wa Slovak. She shook her head, smiling. No, Russian, and she opened up in the way I hope she would, so I invited her over to sit with us.

Martin finally got fed up with the Fiji guy and announced he was leaving, and the other guys went along. Anna and I left together. We walked across Old Town Square. It was ve quiet that evening, we could see by the lights coming down reflected off the cobblestone. was beautiful; Anna murmured quietly about magic Prague, her English was just enough for us to communicate. We kissed standing there on the dark square, like a couple of tourists but not caring, and it was when I kissed her that I first caught the dark madnes in her eyes and how it resolved into a sigh, an ecstasy she was so ready to achieve. It wa look I would come to know pretty well later.

She lived in Dejvice also, not far from Evropska Square, just a couple of tram stops dowr from our place, so we got the night tram at Vodichkova, the tram which would take us b across the river. The tram was full of people heading home from the bars – it was a weeknight – but we didn't notice them. We stood in the back of the tram, our hands reaching up to hold onto the railing and swaying close together, almost as if we were dancing, as the tram began its twisting descent up the hill at Mala Strana on the way pa the park toward Hradcany. Her kisses were very soft, interrupted now and again by the lurch of the tram, and she spoke in a low, murmuring voice. She said she was happy I h seen her looking at me, and her broken, husky English had something mysterious, even dangerous in it. It seemed to promise all the strange, dark places that we would visit. She got off at Evropska Sqare and we agreed to meet there the following evening.

following evening was a windy, very cold night. The big roundabout in Dejvice, pska Avenue, was snowy and silent, windblown. There were a few cars and trams, but air felt curiously quiet and calm. I waited at the tram stop, and when the time came for o come she wasn't there and I thought she wasn't going to come. But then I saw her, isk, long strides, crossing the square. She wore a fancy beige overcoat and her long, ant white-blonde hair was swept back, and her cheeks were flushed with thrilling, ctant formality. It was evident she had composed herself for the evening, and I noticed nadness had been carefully groomed, brushed and put away, and the smile and turned k were those belonging to a Russian woman who wishes to present herself properly to ntleman in the street on a snowy, cold night. I liked it, it was as though she were sha or Sonya or any of the proper mad women of Dostoevsky's novels.

pekt," she coolly corrected me when I attempted a second kiss.

ered an arm, in the old style, and she was pleased and took it. We walked a couple ks to a small, modest restaurant not far from the markets. Anna knew the café, the u, so we ordered a pizza, and beer. We were both a little nervous now, more aware of communication barriers, but with the food and beer we soon relaxed. Anna asked lots uestions, about why I had come to Prague, and what I did in America, and told me a lot She was from Rostov, a city in southern Russia. She'd moved to Prague a few years re and was working as a page designer for an online tourist magazine that catered to ists back in Russia. Because she hadn't yet procured the necessary papers, she was king under the table and living in the country technically illegally.

des these things, I found she, as I expected, was into all manner of astrology, omens, erstitions and things relating to the occult. Numerology, palm-reading. She asked for date of birth, and a few other key figures and I watched her work the numbers, quickly with concentration on her beautiful brow. "You have a very complicated character," said, summarising her calculations. "And for you, what is important – everything must ays be new."

smiled, pleased with her asessment, and her eyes then were happy and calm. The r thing I had seen wasn't there yet. It came a little later, when we had more beer. Then v the madness, as if awakening from a long, luxurious nap, raising and stretching in eyes. But when I walked her home later, she had carefully brushed it and put it away n, for when we reached her flat, she kissed me but insisted on letting herself in.

w nights later, she invited me for dinner, but this time to her apartment. When she wered the door, there was again the carefully displayed formality, but this time she dn't hold it and when she saw me her face lit up, radiant and ravishing and she let me her, her lips were warm and brushed against yours slowly, like a hairbrush passing ugh your hair, and you felt their current, and her hair smelled of powder and a floral ume.

a took my shoes in the foyer, and handed me a pair of slippers. In the kitchen a simple, elegant meal had been prepared, in the Russian style, roasted chicken and boiled atoes with a tasty soup and some greens. She brought beer for my sake, but during the ner she placed a bottle of vodka on the table and like all Russians, she dropped back s during the meal with scarcely a thought, almost indifferently, and refilled my ctant shot glass with an almost insolent challenge.

talked. Again, I won't try to reproduce our conversations because they were too halting, of hand gestures, and nods and corrections, to really make them cohesive. We talked as ples who are getting to know one another do when they're having a nice dinner alone ther. We talked of the food, we talked about each other, we talked about life in Russia, merica, in Prague, and we talked more about ourselves.

r dinner we went into her bedroom. Anna was most at home here, for it was where she nt most of her time, she said. There was the computer where each morning she got up went to work on her pages, there were always deadlines (According to her numerology, said, work for her was "the most important thing"). There was also a big bed with oon blankets and covers. I ended up staying that night, and the bed was a nice change from the converted couch I slept on at our flat. That night – it was bitterly cold out, we could hear the wind blowing – I came to know that look, the gentle madness of it, her madness that was so mad it was gentle, as she opened it up like a present, and it seem to seize her, to suffuse her entire body, like a fever. I caught it too and it was like travel through a vortex at blinding speed, only the feeling was not terror you felt but only a strange calm, as you did laying in a warm bed with a now sleeping lover while listening the snowy, cold wind blow outside.

It was very early when I got up. Outside it was still dark. Anna had to get up soon, she said, but she went back to sleep while I had a shower and dressed. I had to go back to t apartment and pick up my bag and change clothes and go to work.

When I came out of the shower she was still sleeping, her long, white, lovely spent body sleeping like an animal, or a child. I woke her and she put on a robe and walked with m the foyer to let me out. There was a closeness between us that was foreign, an intimacy that was strange, but you accepted it as you did the mint-freshness of the morning. We embarrassed, a need for a separate peace, time to gather.

We went out again a few nights later. This time we got the metro to Namesti Miru. It wa the first time I'd been to that part of Prague, and I have a memory of the big church lit u and the trees in the park. We walked quickly past the park to Vinohrady Avenue, Anna leading the way until we arrived at a bar located down some steps just off the street. Th interior was that cool blue and red lighting some bars have, and there were people but i wasn't crowded. We ordered drinks and sat at a table and talked. That look was in Anna eyes again now that we were in the bar. She told me to look around. I did, but not catch her point, looked back at her. She wanted me to notice. "Only women," she said, gigglin was her surprise for the evening, and I could tell she was waiting to see how I would tak this present. But I'd lived in California for many years, so after I caught her point I saw nothing especially to be surprised about.

My response was unsatisfactory, I could see that. She wanted me to be really surprised. had been shocked, she might have liked it. She wanted to have this secret, like the othe secrets, between us and we would both know about it. But first the values of her world required me to at least be a little surprised. This was not hard to do, and she looked so damn beautiful as always, so I was surprised. She saw me trying and was pleased that I was cooperating. The keen, mad look in her eyes suddenly softened, vanished altogethe and for just a second I saw someone else. Inside their was a child, a little lost girl who wanted to give everything to you because she herself did not know what to do with it. I'd felt that too that night at her apartment, late in the night as she slept beside me. Now, seeing her so happy that I was playing along in the evening's game, I saw again how rea frightened she was, far from home. She'd crossed a meridian, as I had, coming from America, and it was another little secret we had.

Just as quickly, the look passed, and the demon was back.

I am aware that my "liberalism," which has come from years of travel, is for the most pa veil that has proven useful over the years. "Keeping an open mind" about everything not only exposes you to many new people and places and experiences, but even better it allo one to easily account for one's own vagaries. Deep down, I suspect the conservative hab and values of my parents have never really been thrown off. I just learned to ignore then whenever it suited my purposes and appetites.

Whether or not Anna's big secret that night was that she occasionally batted for the oth team was not really important; in California I dated several women who had girlfriends the side, or where ever it is one puts them. I was used to "complicated women," I seeme attract them. No, what I really thought about, watching the madness creep back in behi her smile, was something my father might have said, if he were there: this girl was a handful.

But as I said, I've grown pretty adept at ignoring sensible impulses. Instead I kept lookir at Anna, and listening to her; she was easy to look at. I looked closer, and she let out a little gasp, and the child came back, her blue, wounded-warm eyes, and she seemed to sure me that the other self was still there, but that it was understood between us it was put away for now and that we would both take it out and enjoy it together later, vould be that person together, but later. Her expression told me that I was doing well, ng to understand her, and that I need only continue with that night's little game and in dark later she would show me anything I wanted.

king back, I can say that at that point I'd seen three faces of Anna. There was the al Anna, who wished to present herself in the style suitable to a Russian woman in her ion. There was the mad Anna of the night, and then there was the frightened child a, desperate and lost and so eager to love.

then, as you know, in those days, I was spinning myself, heading in three or four rent directions myself, and so perhaps to Anna I too had faces, was a changeling: naps that was another of our secrets.

unds like I'm really building Anna up, like she was a great love. Actually whether she or simply a missed chance at hell or misery or madness I don't know because I never ly gave her a chance. Communication was a big problem for both of us, and I think we yed having the mystery, which is great for sex but disastrous in a relationship. The k nights were our time, with the cold outside and everything warm within, our bodies hing under the blankets and in the night, the one looking for the other and knowing other was there. We were like visitors in some other country (and we really were) but it ned to us we were mapping a whole new spiritual geography (I suppose that's true for one who's ever been in a cross-cultural relationship); we were creating this new place, was creating itself, and we were its first citizens, afraid and strange and new.

that was in the night. By day we were practically strangers. I worked at the school, elled around Prague to the various companies, and didn't think about Anna at all, and I pose she worked at her computer in the flat and didn't think of me either. Once I ran her by accident at the metro station in Dejvice. We shared a seat and rode to the ter together. She was dressed professionally, and for just a moment let slip our secret le and we both felt self-conscious in the bright morning, seeing our other selves.

e evenings I'd call and her voice would be remote, cold, and I knew she had made other ns. Our conversations were a study in the absence of words. I could picture her on the r end of the line, her beautiful, white-blonde hair flowing in and out of her mad blue s, the sad, full mouth, and I'd want her all over again. So I'd hang up and just forget her go out for another wild night with Martin and Charlie, and in a day or two she would . Her voice was always different when she called than when I called. When she called I w immediately where I was going to be that night. Her voice over the phone then was of night, a whispered night, full of blue silhouettes and mad ghosts peering from the s.

as I said, that was not who we were most of the time – it was too exhausting – and we naps knew there was no point in really getting to know the other parts of ourselves ause they weren't compatible.

the night at Le Clan when I ran into Anna without expecting to. I was sitting at a table nstairs with the guys and it was really late.

ere's Anna," Martin said, and I turned and looked. She was coming down the steps, king in the opposite direction toward the other side of the room. Her hair was lovely, shed smooth down her back, and her lovely figure shone beneath the lights. I could tell was looking for someone, so I got up, rashly, and went up and tapped her on the ulder.

ment!" She said. The music was loud. When she'd turned and recognized me, I could there was no pleasure in seeing me. She went back to scanning the room, almost as if I n't even there. I went back to the table, feeling angry and embarrassed. At Martin's gestion we paid and left.

r that night I resolved I was through with her and her mad games. I was mortified, to nonest, that she'd frozen me out right in front of my friends, and wanted to punish her. l so I made no effort to contact her, and went back to teaching and going out with the guys. A week or so passed. Then one evening, right in the middle of a class, my phone beeped. A message from Anna.

So of course I went and saw her. That evening she prepared another big dinner and was the Anna I knew again, the good Russian woman, the homemaker, the wife, and she loo at me anxiously while I ate, put more food on the plate, filled my vodka glass and lit my cigarettes. I could see she wanted to talk about the night at Le Clan, and was waiting fo me to bring it up, but I didn't bring it up, I finished eating and smoked and waited for h to talk about it.

Finally she did, gingerly filling my glass again. It was her girlfriend, she was waiting to n her girlfriend. I'd guessed that it was either another man or another woman, so Anna sa wasn't surprised. With halting English and lots of hand gestures, Anna tried to make m understand about the girl, how it was really all right, and there was nothing at all for m worry about. It was something between them, just as she and I had something, and it w perfectly all right. As Anna explained all this I thought how nice and reasonable this Anı was, but also about the other Anna I'd seen at Le Clan, and the other Annas. I saw she no control over them, the other Annas, and they were constantly invading her, shifting i her, the currents of her fevered psyche: the faces of Anna that I too well recognized, sinc they were like my own in some ways. She could feel quite deeply toward me, even love m but only at times, like Natasha in "The Idiot." I was her Prince Myshkin. She loved my w "innocent" American eyes, which she said were "very French." She loved that simplicity i me that she thought she alone understood. To her I was a "good man" but I had to understand that Anna was also a good girl who could be many other things too. If I coul understand this about her – she knew I could! lighting my cigarette – then everything would be fine and lovely.

I could see the pitch, but I was very proud and stubborn in those days. When you're you you take your greatness for granted – you resent it when you think it's not being given it proper due.

Anyway, I went along with everything, at least for a while. Looking back, I think I understood Anna's faces, but not my own. I suppose I wanted what most young men do: good sex, no complications.

"But that's so boring!" Anna said this one night during one of our "serious" talks. These had on her computer, using a Google translator, and took turns typing our agonizing thoughts and confessions. She wanted to know all about me, about other women I'd known, and was deeply impressed when I confided that a woman had once broken my heart, and that I'd left America to start life anew. Her feeling were easily touched, and sh thought me a very romantic figure. We talked of her life in Russia, about the longstandir affair she'd had with her boss, a rich businessman from Minsk, and with whom she'd be in love, this when she was very young, she said.

Now there was Zora, the girlfriend. Anna wanted very much for us to meet. She thought we'd really be great friends. We did meet eventually. One Saturday, just as the spring wa coming to Prague, Anna held a birthday party at her flat. Anna was queen of the day, Natasha; she wore a silver tiara over her beautiful head, and was blushing with exciteme all afternoon. The girlfriend, Zora, and I were introduced as soon as I arrived. She was a short, stocky, almost humpbacked creature who was neither rude nor polite, regarding r with a quick, indifferent nod, and quietly returned to preparing the meal. Anna helped Z with the preparations, while at the same time running to answer the door to let in more guests. Most of them were Russians who lived in the city, and greeted Anna with hugs a kisses and great well wishes for her birthday. Most of them didn't speak English, but the made an effort to be interested and polite. Anna was conscious of my discomfort – the ot guests all were chatting gaily together in Russian or Czech – and brought me a beer and patted my shoulder, before running back to the kitchen or the answer the door. I tried to sit back and avoid any notice, to just drink beer and enjoy the atmosphere. A couple of Anna's gay friends from the discos showed up. We'd met one night, Anna had wanted m meet her friends, and it had been a strange evening; they were jealous and made little

:ing remarks all evening. But at the party that day they were polite, even glad to see I think Anna must have said something to them after that other evening. Anyway, the guys at least spoke English and so I had someone to talk to while Anna whirled about flat.

ia's invitation had come unexpectedly (she hadn't told me her birthday was coming), so dn't even bought her a gift. Instead, I brought along my guitar, along with the lyrics to ng I'd been toying with and now hastily rearranged into the semblance of a ballad. I ight if nothing else, Anna would find a birthday song different.

guitar was noticed by the other guests a bit later, after the meal was served and yone had eaten and were putting away beer and vodka like true Russians and the party really starting to pick up. Anna had been busy with her friends all afternoon and didn't e time to spend with me. It was her day so I didn't begrudge her, and tried to just talk i the gay guys, drink beer and let Anna have her birthday the way she wanted to.

n somebody asked about the guitar. Others noticed it too and so they put it in my ds and asked me to play. So I figured this was a good time for Anna's birthday song. I an to strum it – it was a slow ballad – and the chords floated through the smoky room. ia was talking with some friends, but she stopped talking, everyone stopped talking and ned. It was a pretty easy song, and I wish I could remember some of the lyrics but ember I'd hastily penned them that afternoon and after that day I never played it again, 've forgotten. Everyone could see I was playing for Anna and they listened respectfully, i Russian appreciation for emotion, sincerity and music. Tears welled in Anna's eyes, py tears, unbelieving tears – no one had ever written a song for her! – and naturally I wed up midway through, I should have practiced it a couple more times. Everyone tended not to notice, and I got through the rest of it. Anna's eyes flickered with appointment, dismay, but everyone filled it in with enthusiastic applause and glasses e raised to Anna and to me and everyone clinked glasses and I played a couple more gs. Anna brightened again with the toasts and cheers and music and was happy; after it was novelty, and she always craved that.

netime later that afternoon, I became aware of another man at the party. I don't know he was, I suppose another friend of Anna's. He greeted me with sullen, almost ressive courtesy. He asked what I was doing in Prague, how I had met Anna, and so on. uely, I wondered if he too had some relationship with Anna, was a rival, but I didn't it to ask. The man, his name was Pavel, became more courteous as the party went on, it was an uncomfortable courtesy. I suspected he was patronizing me, feeling I were a fect fool who he felt needed to be humoured for Anna's benefit. Perhaps Anna had even ched him beforehand.

ryone was getting pretty drunk by then, and the room got noisier and smokier. People appeared, went in and out of the rooms, and you heard their voices in the other rooms. sic pumped non-stop from the stereo. Zora went about in her quiet, hunch-backed way, king up empty plates. I was drunk, most people were, and hadn't seen Anna for a while, o it seemed. I was bored, and resentful. People were at that point when the party must on, so it did, everyone had forgotten about me. I found myself picking up the guitar and ig to the foyer to put on my shoes. Anna suddenly appeared in the doorway, blocking exit. In one hand she held a glass of vodka, and the tiara had slipped and sat at a oked angle, and her eyes were drunk and wild. She kissed me passionately, hungrily, it was a messy, alcohol kiss and I brushed past her and left.

w months passed. Summertime came, a loud, warm, languid summer. The trams were full with sweating tourists. I was on the number 26 tram from Hradcanska to ossmayerovo Namesti when I suddenly noticed Anna. She was sitting near the front king out the window. It was the first time I'd seen her since the party, since afterward I'd sorry about messing up her birthday party and hadn't tried to contact her.

looked around and saw me. I was expecting her to turn away angrily. But instead the s that met mine were startled, then happy.

iat is new with you?" she asked.

Nothing much was actually. By then Martin and Charlie had already left Prague, the schools were having a slow summer, and I was finding the going pretty rough. I had four some freelance work with the Czech Business Weekly and a few private students, but ot than that, was struggling to pay the rent. The wild nights in the center already seemed l ago.

Anna was got off before I did, but before she did she gave me her card (I'd lost my phone and had to replace it) and told me to call her again. For whatever reason, I never did.

of the weekend

young women at Club Paradise, Darling and Atlas were all good-looking, some were beautiful. Most of them came from the East; Ukraine , Russia , the Baltic states . They ally came to Prague , so the story went, with a boyfriend or husband who pushed the into the nightclub scene with the ambitions of the girl making them both a lot of ey. I don't know if this story is true – maybe true for some – and I know Kristina and a others I met told me they were students paying their way through university, which have been true too. It could be the women claimed to have boyfriends or husbands at e merely as protection from the hordes of drunken, pill-popping sex tourists, many of m wanted more than just the paid half hour upstairs. These drunken guys, fueled by asy, drink and frustration, overheated by the rhythms of the discos, would go upstairs half an hour later convince themselves they were in love, and would set out to save the maiden from her sordid situation.

girls generally took such offers the same way each time: the suitor would be ouraged to come back and spend more of his money. They were very sweet about it, the , and were very warm and tender – usually – as long as you were spending your money. u didn't spend money they were offended and turned mean pretty quickly. Who could ne them? The unsubtle hint was, do you really think I'd be wasting my time with you if weren't going to pay?"

nember one time, Martin and I went to the Paradise Club. He had already left Prague hen and was just back for a visit. We'd done our usual rounds in Chateau and Le Clan Studio that weekend and now it was Sunday night and he was leaving for Donegal in morning. He'd met one of the girls out at Studio that morning and got her number and d promised to meet him sometime if her mother was feeling better. This was another y: the mum was always ill and needed looking after.

t was Sunday night and Martin was leaving in the morning and he wanted to go to the adise Club and try to meet this girl; I went along for support.

as slow, since it was Sunday. All the tourists and businessmen had already flown back was during the height of the Easyjet.com cheap flights, which made a weekend in gue cheaper and more fun than staying home in London or Dublin, so every weekend les of guys and men would descend on the city in search of cheap beer and pills and sex). At the club most of the tables were empty, except for one stag party consisting of or five guys. A girl with lovely tawny hair and honey-colored skin was doing a table ce. Up on the stage a girl was dancing, and the other girls watched and sat desultorily ne tables and took turns dancing. When one girl finished she came off the stage, her e body passing nimbly by the tables while another girl went up.

Martin and I ordered a beer (250 crowns each) and sat at one of the empty tables and watched the dance and talked about the weekend. Martin kept sending text messages t the girl. It appeared she would meet him but she had to wait for her mother to go to sle While we waited some of the girls came and sat with us. The were all damned good-look in their light dresses. They all had the same, practiced approach and by then I'd been a times and had developed the same practiced answers.
A typical "conversation" went like this:
"Do you like me?"
"Of course. You're beautiful."
"I'm beautiful?"
"Of course."
"So you want to go upstairs? Private dance? I do anything you want."
"I would love to go upstairs or anywhere with you."
"So you want? Let's go."
"I would love to. But I can't. Not tonight."
"Not tonight? Why not? You don't like me?"
"I like you. But I'm just waiting for my friend. He is meeting somebody."
"Your friend?"
"Yes, my friend there." I indicate Martin, who is having a similar conversation with a similar girl.
"You and your friend are not gay? We can go upstairs. Anything you want."
You can't help but smile and kind of sigh. She is good-looking, and soft, and the illusior not bad, even tender somehow, as the tenderness itself is an illusion.
:"Next time," you say.
"Next time? When? You come tomorrow? When do you go back to England ?"
"I'm not from England . America ."
" America . Are you on holiday?'
"No. I live in Prague ."
"So you come tomorrow?"
"Maybe."
She's already getting up and she gives a parting smile and then, as though there were a signal, another girl comes over and sits down. It's a slow night, and on a slow night mar will sit down. The night before, with all the tourists and businessman still there, and yo would have gotten no such attention. But they've still got to make their money so tonigh you're gonna get a lot of it. Meanwhile, Martin and I drink our beers slowly and try to watch the dance.
Then one of the girls comes back, a raven-haired, tan beauty who had sat with me earli She's not so nice this time.
"You know this is not a cinema," she says, an edge in her voice. "If you want to just look to the cinema."
There are variations. Others will say: it's not just a bar, or if you say you are waiting for someone, well, why don't you wait outside? Anyway, the message was the same and you hated to hear it after the girls had been so nice. For some reason that evening I took it t wrong way. I mean, I knew the routine, and one could not blame the girls. It was how th were instructed by their bosses, and we wanted nothing to do with their bosses. The ma controlled many of the clubs downtown then.
I knew all of this but that night, it being Martin's last night, I got a bit bent out of shape "We're just sitting here having a beer," I told the girl. "Why can't you leave us alone? Wh don't you leave?"
I think this reply surprised the girl a bit, she generally thought we were nice guys, and I English wasn't really that good except for the routine questions and answers, so it's possible she didn't quite understand. But the tone of the words and my manner she understood perfectly, for she kind of froze up and skittered away. A few minutes later I s her standing with the other girls fuming and cursing violently.

ne on, let's go," Martin said. There was a note of urgency in his voice.
ıght what he meant and we both rose to pay. We were both imagining some goon in a k suit emerging from the shadows, ready to take us outside and beat the shit out of us. nothing happened and we paid and left.
on Wenceslas Square it was drizzling and wet and beat. The weekend was over. The ks selling sausages and coffee were slow, and only a few of the Gypsy girls were out. :? Sex?" they asked in mechanical voices. A young man passed. "Charlie? Charlie?" :h was the slang for drugs. We never bought from these guys, but Martin liked to tease n.
v much?" he asked.
). One gram."
.lshit!" Martin suddenly seemed tired. "I lived here for two years and I know the price gram of marijuana is 250 crowns."
walked off. Martin had lived in Prague for only six months. It was I who by then was g on two years, but I understood why he added that in. He was tired and feeling ancholy – he was still waiting to see that girl. We both felt tired, filled with that peration and loneliness that comes after two many lost sunrises at Studio and Le Clan Paradise; tired of feeling like amped-up ghosts, silhouettes, targets for scams and we tired of the sudden hardness of whores who had been so soft and tender before. But it more than that, the catch of despair in Martin's voice I thought I recognized as my : the feeling that no matter how well you thought you had gotten to know the city, that would never belong there.
nat moment, Martin got a message and it was the girl. She wanted to meet him and ld meet him at the Powder Tower around midnight. Martin asked if I wanted to go but I an early class in the morning, and by then it was already past eleven. I knew he had early flight too but he didn't care, he would just stay up and sleep on the plane.
ne drizzling late-hour lamplight near Vodichkova Street we shook hands and promised ee each other again soon. I would even get over to see him and the other guys in egal.
ıh, I'll call you when I get in," he said. He smiled his Donegal grin. "Besides, this bitch o'ly won't turn up. It's just as well. Stay black, man!" The last was just a silly saying we
tram was coming, so I got on and as it pulled away toward Charles Square I saw tin, walking the opposite direction down Jindriska Street, making his way over to the der Tower.

The Murder of Winter

OK, so we left Martin alone on Jindriska Street late at night on his way to meet that girl turns out all right so we don't have to worry about him. Let us move forward just for a moment a few years, and return again to Donska Street, the street where I spent my las year in Prague.

There is a day celebrating St. Nikolas when young Czechs, especially children, dress up angels and devils. You see them in the metro stations or walking along the windy streets Usually it's the girls who dress as angels and the men as devils. The girls wear little win sewn onto the backs of white sheets, and they spray sparkles in their hair and put their hair up in elaborate ways. The men wear horns and black sheets and sometimes some d make-up. Every now and then you see a guy and girl who have switched roles, and sometimes you see a combination, like a girl with wings and devil horns. I always liked t combination the best.

I liked it because for me it expressed what I like about Czech humor, the dark, playful subversive side of the Czech personality. Bohemia is an old culture, dating back to the 8 or 9th Century, but the modern Czech Republic is essentially an adolescent, and you se in those young people dressed as angels and devils, carrying very old traditions on in a young republic.

It was winter then, but still early winter, near Christmas when winter is full of festivity a charm. But then the weeks pass and the winter gets harder and deeper, and it seems lik no other season ever existed. When these days came, sometimes it would be raining and snowing at the same time. My Czech friends would say, "The Devil is getting married today." It was an old Bohemian folk saying, and hearing it reminded me that underneat the modern Republic are the other layers of history, and then the country's image to me changed back from a playful adolescent dressed in a costume to that of an old village woman crossing herself while evil passed outside.

Then there was *masopust*. This happened somewhere in the middle of the winter, just w it got its bleakest and hardest, when the snow was knee-deep in someplaces and the windshields of cars were smashed by falling ice cycles, and you could not walk down Donska Street without slipping on the ice, and could never feel warm. The snow would b hard-packed and the air lifeless and brittle and grey.

Then suddenly, you're walking to the park at the foot of Krymska Street and hear music You follow the sound of the music, some old Moravian folk tune on a violin or guitar, an the sound leads you to a park at the foot of the street. People are having a barbecue. You see David from Shakespeare and Sons and lots of other people from the neighborhood.

ryone is dressed in their parkas and gloves and scarves, and a few people are dressed ostumes. A man is barbecuing sausages and a woman is handing out hot wine and r. You pay for a sausage and a hot wine, served in a plastic cup. You go and listen to music. The sausage tastes hot and smoky, and it warms you, as does the wine. You ask id what was going on and he says, “We are having a masopust. It means “meat fast.We trying to murder the winter.”

d a bit of research later and found that it was part of the Lent, and many countries have ilar festivities, except they are called carnivals, like in Brazil . After eating the sausage, I ned to the music some more and finished the wine, then trudged back up the hill to kespeare and Sons. Inside it was warm. Then some of the masopusters came and sat in r costumes at the bar. We all ordered drinks. They were taking turns having breaks. It Saturday afternoon and winter had a long ways to go, but it was cozy that afternoon in kespeare's with the masopust people, and I sat and drank a beer and watched them e turns coming in to get warm.

member it was two, maybe three days later, but the winter broke. The snow melted, the hillsides appeared again, and the sun came out. It wasn't spring, but the worst of the ter was definitely gone. You knew it. I went outside and it was warmer than it had been there was a faint fresh smell that comes when the weather changes. I thought about masopust in the park, the people in their costumes and sausages and music, and hed them well.

Car-kicking and other adventures

There are important lessons to be drawn from kicking a car going full speed down a narr street at night while drunk and returning home from the pub in a foreign city.

First, when you kick the car, be prepared to be catapulted into the air, jerked and floppe around like a bizarre marionette, like clothing drying in the rippling wind, by the force o the passing car. Then you hit the concrete.

Second, if you actually succeed in kicking the car passing at full speed, and have surviv make sure you disappear in a hurry, hide somewhere, because the owner of the car is going to circle back around the block and come looking to beat your ass, while his girlfriend in a panic calls the police on her mobile.

Finally, when the police arrive, make sure there is enough money in your bank account that you can hastily find a Bankomat to pay off the driver. That way you avoid getting arrested, paying a big fine anyway, and later, having your visa renewal application reject on account of your 'criminal record.'

All of the above are valid and true lessons, drawn from actual events. I know because it happened to me, the January night I tangoed with a sleek, black Skoda on Sokolovska Street in Karlin. Karlin is a neighbourhood not far from Namesti Republiky, and has in recent years been home to major redevelopment. I was living there in a small converted house just across the street from Karlinska Namesti.

That night I'd been out having drinks with another American teacher. We drank our usu fill, which was too much, and parted and I walked back through Namesti Republiky and toward the Florenc metro station and on under the railway overpass to the neighborhoo Karlin.

The funny thing, is that night I was just a few hundred meters from my flat. I mean, this might never have even happened. My flat, as I said, was just across the street from Karlinska Namesti, which had a lovely park full of trees and just beyond a big beautiful neoclassical church. By then it was getting a bit late, but most of the shops and cafes we still open. Now, understand that when I drink I tend to withdraw into myself at some poi ruminate, stew, philosophize, remember, forget: a lot goes on. That night I was chewing something, the alcohol had taken its turn, and anger was beginning to work its way through my veins.

Suddenly, down Sokolovska Street – it's a really long, straight street – a black car with it headlights shining, came roaring down the street. It was moving way too fast for such a ow street. Often this happened in Prague and by day it annoyed me. Prague's streets not designed for Formula One racing.

vay why I was in the road to begin with is not worth going into. I was drunk. As the car oached, I directed all my intoxicated anger at the car, and as it passed, I somehow ched myself, like Chuck Norris, and landed a kick into the side of the car as it passed. avy, rib-crunching thud found me on the street, stunned, staring up at the night sky, cond or two later.

nge to say, I just got up, a little unsteadily, but still numbed enough by the beer to not y feel any pain, and just kept walking home. I was about one hundred meters away my flat. It didn't even occur to me that I'd done anything out of the ordinary. If it had, bably would have picked up the pace, or, even better, ducked across the street into the and found refuge among the trees and the night gypsies, and perhaps following the lows went out past the church and over to the Zizkov tunnel, if I could make it that far. could have gone down toward the Vltava and hid along its banks.

I was too drunk for any of that. Instead, I just kept walking, the impact of hitting the ment had been enough to knock the inebriated anger out of me. I walked as in a daze. didn't notice until it was too late the black car suddenly passing again, screeching to a , and a voice yelling in my direction. The driver, a young man, popped his head out of car, saw me, shouted again and got out of the car and came straight toward me. He cked me, and shouted some more, in English. I think it was obvious to him I was ık. He pulled me over to the car, and bending down, showed me a dent (small to me, to him). The girlfriend had got out of the car too and was rushing around speaking to ple and pointing at me. I wanted to just turn away and go home but no one would let eave. A taxi driver, a heavyset man, who'd either seen it or had just heard the story decided to side with the driver, stood in my path. A young gypsy man, who didn't k a word, was trying to quietly sneak me away from the scene, but people saw he was g this and stopped him.

ı the police arrived.

sport!" one of them demanded. I didn't have it with me, so they took my driver's license ead. My name, as all legal foreigners, was registered with the foreign police.

s taken to the local precinct, just a few blocks away, and put in a cell. The driver by had calmed down, now that the authorities were involved. I think he kind of regretted ng the police involved, but then that was his girlfriend (girlfriends!). He felt we could e everything ourselves. He kept saying, over and over, as they put me in the cell and ed the door, just to pay him 10,000 crowns. "Just give me 10,000 crowns! 10,000!" he saying this, almost pleading. The problem was I didn't have 10,000 crowns. Two emen were there, and as the door was closing I suddenly began to freak out – the hol was still shifting inside me – and for some reason I began calling out for Svejk, the of the famous Czech novel. "Svejk! Svejk!" I cried over and over. Until one of the ers, a big, strong fellow, grabbed both my shoulders and, looking me square in the eye, ok me until I calmed down. Then they left and shut the door.

t later they took me to a hospital to get a blood sample. When they took off my shirt, I ced there were big, ugly purple bruises around my ribs from the fall. The doctor took a k look, snorted and walked off. After they took the sample, I was taken back to the inct where I was booked, fingerprinted, mug-shot. I admit I cried a little as they were ng my photo – the drunkard's moment of maudlin clarity – my great Prague adventure come to this! – and the officers felt a little bad, but they were just doing their job.

of them was about my age, and was really youthful in his features and demeanor. We ed a little while in the back of the car on the way from the hospital. You could tell he ıght I was OK. He was curious about my teaching English, and about America, and I had come to Prague. Yes, I told him. Prague was beautiful, I liked it very much. You ld see he was trying to piece it all together, how someone with my background, cation and apparent qualifications had ended up in this bizarre situation.

I was very curious to know this myself. We both sat and puzzled over it as the car reached the precinct station, but neither of us could reach a satisfactory conclusion. No long after this, there was a story in the Czech news about a local police officer who fatal stabbed an American businessman while they were drinking at the pub. Apparently the been having an argument. In the news report, other police officers tried to defend the assailant. They said that under sober circumstances, this would never have happened. could relate to that.

Back at the precinct it was very late, and most of the staff had gone home for the night. was to spend that night in jail and in the morning a translator would arrive and they co take my statement.

The young officer escorted me from the car back to my cell. On the way in I asked if I co have a cigarette. They'd already confiscated my cigarettes, along with my wallet and oth small possessions for processing. The young officer went and found my cigarettes and le me have one. We went out a side door and while he stood by, I smoked, looking out at t dull, silent late night. When I finished, he took me back to the cell.

In the morning, the translator came, a blousy, intelligent young woman. I was taken downstairs into an office. A different officer was working. He was a swarthy fellow, his s unbuttoned to show a gold chain hiding beneath a hairy chest. As he typed my stateme he also interrogated me in Czech, and the woman translated. When I got to the part abo the car-kicking, he stopped typing and asked many questions, from different angles. Th translator told me the officer had a hard time believing my story. He didn't see how it wa humanly possible for someone, especially someone in my condition, could have manage kick a car passing at the speed I estimated. It was impossible, he said. Ne mozny, you could hear him thinking.

I informed him that perhaps it was hard to believe, but in fact it was true. Looking back realize now that perhaps I should have agreed with the officer. I could have said, yes! Th exactly what I mean, too, officer! These people are lying! It was the car that struck me, r the car! And so on. I could have lifted my shirt and shown him the bruised ribs. But the had already told the other officers on the night shift the whole story. I suppose I could t next day have contradicted that story – after all, I was drunk!

That's what happens when you get arrested. You become like a caged animal, and inste of thinking about what you did wrong, you only think about how you could have avoide being caught. The guilt comes much later.

Once, when I was a teen-ager, some friends and I got caught stealing clothes from a loca mall. We were caught by the security just as we were leaving. The thing was, we'd had a pretty successful haul that afternoon and were already leaving, but decided to go to just one more shop. It was a shop where one of the guys' sister worked. While we went there and talked to her, one of the guys stole a pair of jeans. She noticed the jeans were gone alerted security, and that's how we all got caught. We'd separated, but the police had descriptions and they caught us all and took us all downtown.

Later at the city jail, the other inmates listened to the story and for the next hour or so I discussing it from all the different angles, of how we could have used this tactic or that strategy. You get like that – it passes the time – but of course in the end you eventually, hopefully, come around to realizing what you did – some don't.

For several years in California I worked as a journalist, and spent part of that time cover criminal courts. Every day I'd go over to the courthouse and listen in on some of the cas Every morning, after the day's edition hit the newsstands, I'd come into the news room a my phone would be lit up with messages. Every now and then I'd have messages from inmates housed down at the county jail. Their messages were indignant, unbelieving, wounded, at my "lies" how I was "making things up" that they were innocent. "The jail is always full of innocent men," was my editor's cynical reply.

I understood, on a certain level, where these guys were coming from. I'd been there, pt for in most cases these guys were up for a lot more than stealing clothes. But tever the crime, there are consequences. Some can accept them, others can't. an, if you were looking at twenty five years to life in prison, possibly even the death alty, wouldn't you fight? And if the newspapers printed stories detailing, in grisly ion, the allegations that you plunged a knife into your uncle's chest, killing him almost antly, in an argument over money and drugs, wouldn't you protest: it wasn't like that! t's not me!

ew how it went, but learned to steel myself against it. So that morning, sitting in the inct station, I thought for a second or two about lying, of changing my story, but then sed on it. I didn't want the hassle, or to be like one of those guys back at the county jail. ial is a huge waste of time and spirit. I just wanted to get out.

hat morning I finished giving the statement. The translator asked me if I wanted to ude in the statement that I was sorry, I said, yes. I was sorry. They went and gave me k my wallet and cigarettes and driver's license and I was allowed to leave, awaiting fication of a date to appear in court. Outside it was a chilly morning, but there was no w. I walked back through the streets. It was Saturday morning and very quiet. At the I crashed for several hours, since the night before I'd slept badly in the cell. But free! e!

Suricate Smile

Around the time of my car-kicking escapade I was seeing Elizabeta. Beta was from a sm city in the High Tatry mountains of Slovakia, but who had come to Prague for better opportunities. When I met her she'd been in Prague about a decade, was in her late twenties, and working as an au pair for a wealthy Italian businessman, his wife and the two young children.

Beta and I met through a mutual friend one afternoon at the Literary Café near Tyn Church. It was a Saturday afternoon, and I had gone there to read, and was winding my way through a second reading of Turgenev's Fathers and Sons, when I noticed the mutu friend and Beta sitting at the next table. "You looked like an intellectual," Beta teased m later. "Reading that depressing Russian literature in a café. Me? I couldn't imagine doin that. Going to a café just to read a book."

We took to each other almost immediately though, and our mutual friend must have noticed this, for she excused herself and said she had to meet some people, and left us alone together. Several hours later, with evening coming to Old Town, we found ourselve holding hands ("What's this?" Beta asked teasing again, looking down at our hands) and heading to Slovansky dum to catch Jiri Menzel's new film which had just opened. It was adaption of Hrabal's "I Served the King of England."

It was a very pleasant evening. Being an admirer of both Hrabal and Menzel, I was excite about the prospect of watching the film in Czech, and with my new companion Beta. I'd read the book and knew the story well enough to follow the film, but Beta would transla now and again. She watched the film intently, and occasionally I turned and looked at h in the ghost-blue light of the cinema. She was perky, alert, with almond-shaped brown e and rich, thick dark hair cut short. Best of all were her warm, robust lips, which parted into a very winning smile, and she smiled often. She thought her nose rather thick, a Russian nose, but it went well with her face and I didn't notice it, except in as it went we with the rest of her.

We sat close during the film, and occasionally she turned and gave me a kiss, like we we teen-agers, and we'd turn back to the film. "Pozor!" she'd whisper.

disagreed on the film (we were often to disagree on such things). I merely enjoyed the erience of being able to follow a director and writer, whose work I admired, in a story in their native language, a cultural experience. My critical sense was turned off. Beta, he other hand, dismissed the work as hardly Menzel's best effort, pointing out the ly brisk editing, the Hollywood-ness of the techniques used. Pointing out one of the ty actresses in the film: "Hm! The Czech Scarlett Johannson!" was her derisive remark. w her points but silently held my own counsel, not wishing to spoil our building port.

following weekend, I believe it was, the first hard snows came to Prague (and only hard ws, as it turned out to be a very light winter). Beta called and invited me over to her flat lunch. She lived in Skalka, on Prague's outskirts, in a flat she shared with two ainian girls. The girls were employed in one of the souvenir shops in Old Town, and e working that day.

the bus ride across town, through Zizkov and out past Strasnice I was in a good mood, ching the snow fall on the grey streets. I was in a good mood because I knew we were ng to make love.

a was busying preparing the lunch when I arrived. It was a modest, small flat in an old alaky with not much in the way of a view, but Beta had cheered it up with her sonality and resourcefulness. Lively cello music issued from a CD player, and in the hen were fresh vegetables, the makings of a salad, which we started on. We ate without aking much, Beta could shift from very gay and lively to quiet very suddenly, we moved to a pasta dish and drank glasses of red wine. After lunch with scarcely a word we went ner bedroom, undressed and made love. It was very natural and nice, and afterward, we ne back out to the living room and sat for a while on the sofa, finishing off the lunch e. "Now that you've got what you wanted you're very quiet," she said. I was quiet. I ked at her and her eyes shined with a hurt, lonesome kind of love, and so I kissed her l we went back to the bedroom and made love again.

re are some places, and certain times of year, that are better for making love than ers, just as you can enjoy wine more at some times than others. For me, winter is the t time for love-making, it is a time for closeness, the warmth of human touch, and for delicious cozy nap afterward under the warm blankets. Beta had the Slovak's natural for hospitality ("Which we never get back!" was always her retort), especially those from smaller towns. As we lay together, Beta would sigh as I stroked her fox-tail thick dark r, the side of her smooth cheeks, her sleeping eyelids. The afternoon took on a blank, ished quality. Somewhere outside in the snow, people were beating their way, bustling e and there under the grey sky, or at best sitting in one of the pubs enjoying beer and ching the hockey matches. All of that was remote, irrelevant, wasted motion. Here was real business of living, the two of us lying together that grey Saturday winter afternoon.

a was not happy in the flat, she told me. The two Ukrainian girls hated her, owing to ty girl grudges ("You leave the window open!"), and she hated them back ("They are like ouple of hyenas! All they do is sit and watch TV when they are home. They say to me, w, Beta! Today we had a salad – and wine!' and I say, 'Yes, so? I have wine and a salad the time!"). She was looking for a new place, but meanwhile she was content to stay over ny place in Karlin when we weren't working. Friday nights were the best time, since we h worked all week, so we'd start to miss each other. Then Friday would come and I'd go l meet her at the tram stop at Karlin Square. She would always have an mp3 player with and she'd pull the plugs out of her little ears in time to say, 'Ahoj!" and we'd kiss like hadn't seen each other for years. Sometimes she'd bring her lap top along so we could ch movies. Still excited, we'd stop at the Vietnamese potraviny and pick up snacks and e and beer for me, and we'd go to my place. My flatmates then were all students and ually went home to their towns on the weekends, so we had the place to ourselves. We'd ke love, then lay around for awhile, eating the snacks and drinking the wine. Then later d shower and dress and head out for the evening. The thing was we were both easy to entertain, and liked that in one another: a movie at Slovansky dum, a walk up to the castle at Hradcany on a sunny afternoon, she liked long walks, or a trip to the zoo to see the giraffes and suricates. The suricates were Beta's favourite. They stood on their hind legs, their slim, curvy bodies swaying, and the big cartoon smiles on their eager faces, re crowd-pleasing grins. I saw why Beta liked them so much, there was something of them her too – she was a bit of an oddball, but attractive all the same, beautifully odd. I called Beta my suricate ("Surukate," I think in Czech) and she was pleased I had given her a nickname, and I was pleased with her.

It was usually Beta who decided where we would go and I generally was content to follow to let her show me around. She'd been living in Prague longer and spoke Czech (Czech a Slovak are similar but not the same), and she enjoyed the role of pointing out things and people and taking us places. It was the au pair in her, I suppose. Sometimes that side of her came out with me, and it could get annoying but generally I tried not to notice, since she was so kind. She corrected my misconceptions, misunderstandings, cast doubt on some of my tastes, smoothed the front of my jacket if it got mussed, fussed, petted, tease me for my American failings, until sometimes I would get annoyed and say something ba But she was easily hurt then, and I'd be sorry.

"What did you eat today, Jamesiku?" she'd ask, using the Slav ending to names that is similar to baby talk. "A hamburger? Why am I not surprised. Americans! You don't know how to take care of yourselves. How many cigarettes did you smoke, Jamesiku? How ma beers? Did you get the new bag you said you were going to get? Your old one looks terrib How –"

But she wasn't always like that. She would also tell me of the two Italian children she looked after, of their progress, their developing personalities, their misbehavior and how she'd corrected them, and I could tell she enjoyed children. That summer, Beta said, she was going to go with the family to Rome and she was counting the days. I admit that jarr seeing as we had just met, that she was looking forward to Rome as something apart, an was a bit jealous. In response, sometimes I would take to criticizing her, for no apparent reason, unreasonably, and she would suddenly look at me, tears in her eyes, all surprise the tears running down her suricate smile, and I would be sorry immediately, and would some way to divert us. She was a good sport, a mountain girl, you could say, and when s saw me doing this she would instantly cheer up.

The night after the car-kicking adventure, we met for a drink at Ferdinand, not far from main train station. Usually we met on Friday nights and since we hadn't that night she wanted to know what had happened. My face got very hot, and I drank a beer and told h everything, how I'd kicked the car, been arrested and spent the night in jail and was now having to go to court. Beta listened very closely, her eyes never leaving mine, watching fo the lie, I think, as women do. When she saw it didn't come, when it was just the story, h face shown in a way I hadn't seen it before, not even after making love. It was a face full ... gratitude! I think for simply telling the truth. It suddenly to me seemed a very small thing too, the whole business, and I wasn't worried anymore. When I finished telling the story, Beta leaned very close and kissed me more warmly than she ever had before, and felt glad, happy. It was almost like going through the night before had been worth it. Her eyes had an assurance in them that everything was going to be all right.

It wasn't, of course. But that night, sitting in Ferdinand, we had a perfect understanding or perfect intimacy, or both. "Milachka." My love. I never called her that. She was my smiling suricate. It sounds corny but she was, and she was content to be that at least fo the time being.

It's not really true, I think, that girls like the bad boy. What the girl really likes is his vulnerability, that with a little coaxing and patience, the good man will emerge from his shell. Delusional as I could be in those days, I waged a quiet rebellion at Beta's efforts to reform me. I mean, like her, I also believed I was a "good man," (ha!) But the difference w I refused to see I could also behave very badly, or that a simple apology for such behavio enough. I acted the part of the spoiled young prince, who sees a night out on the pissing up the walls as his due, "sowing the wild oats." He sees no reason why he ıld change, nor why others should point out his, shall we say, ass-holishness, or olery. Asshole he may be, but a royal asshole, mind you, one entitled to certain ledges. Seriously! Looking back, I never consciously thought like that, but my actions perceptions spoke for themselves. I would be the first to denounce arrogance in ciple, but in practice I was an accomplished expert.

rst, this lurked in the background, safely out of sight. As Beta warmly kissed me that ing at Ferdinand, though I was thankful and responded to her sympathy, in the back y mind was the sneaking suspicion that Beta's sympathy was wasted, that she had yet e the real me, and that worse, she would yet.

said, she was always looking after me, inquiring about my day, what I had eaten, quick ick her tongue in disapproval and offer sensible corrections. To please her, at the café I d sometimes order a cup of tea, two cups, and would drink them instead of beer, while smiled in approval, mock astonishment ("Tea? Something healthy? I am shocked, esiku!") or during our long walks up at the castle or by the Vltava I would make a point ot smoking, and she would notice it and be pleased. She'd sensibly point out that one to think about one's health, especially if one wanted to settle down one day to a wife family. Of course she was right, and naturally it annoyed me. In those days I was the adventurer, the hero of my own drama, and thought the hero should be able to do t damn well pleased him. Health! Wives! Family! A hero needs not such things. They conventional, safe, dull, unsuitable for special people like me. Yes, I considered myself special, I was saving myself for all the great things I was going to accomplish. Didn't understand that?

t" was another sensitive area. We never talked about it much. I don't think she really ght about it that much, my desire to write, I mean. She was too focused on her own gs: the two Italian children who took up her time, as well as the big trip to Rome that coming in the summer. She'd chatter during our walks about the places she had been other places where she wanted to go.

ıst finished a novel around that time, a complete draft. It was not a good novel, but I 't know that then. But it was my first novel and I was very proud of it. I had worked all previous, long winter on it and through the spring and summer before finally reaching t seemed a good ending in the fall. Now the draft sat on the desk, its fresh thickness, the title and my name handsomely displayed at the top, gave me no end of pleasure. was coming out of the shower one evening, I caught Beta peeking at the draft. She ped when I came into the room and I could tell she was curious just from the sheer of the draft, the crispness of the pages.

you like me?" Beta asked one evening as we lay together in the dark. It was spoken in a lonely way, almost as if she were asking the question to herself. I told her of course, I asked if she liked me. "Sometimes," she said, her answer was again wan, flat.

ourse there were many good times. We could walk for hours through the city. Spring e early to Prague that year, and the streets were full of friendly rays of sunshine and all g the banks of the Vltava were the charming fresh smells of flowers and trees in bloom. ne was in any hurry. Just being in Prague on those days was enough for anybody, and ave someone like Beta with you, it just seemed natural, everyone on such spring rnoons had someone. Our kisses, our hands clasped together, they were everybody's es and everybody's hands. It was OK to act a little spoiled, like children, because no anywhere in the city was lonely.

ıe evening we'd go to places like the Cherna Kochka ("The Black Cat") near the Zizkov ıel, or one of the nicer cafes down near the river. Our favourite dish together *bramborachky*, which were potato pancakes, and shots of slivovice, the strong brandy, ve to Slovakia, and is made fresh from pears or plums. The Cherna Kockha had really l bramborachky and slivovice, and it was cozy there, with its low stone ceiling and dark, firelit atmosphere. At the Cherna Kochka you could feel hidden away like a spy ar it felt romantic. You could entertain fantasies that somewhere in the city some killers w pursuing you, and the Cherna Kochka was a safe haven where nobody could find you, except your girl, of course. So it was a good place to take your girl and have a quiet, goc dinner and be alone together talking and putting away a few pints of beer and shots of slivo. Like most Slovaks, Beta could down the slivo shots with a quick flick of the wrist. barmen there all liked her and were very friendly. It charmed them to hear the Slovak accent, which Czechs find softer and more musical than Czech, especially when spoken a pretty young woman. I could tell they thought I, a *cizinec*, was lucky to be with such a nice girl, and it made me feel proud.

One time, to impress her, and because Beta wanted me to pick a place for a change, I tc her to Himalaya, an Indian food restaurant I liked on Soukenicka Street near Namesti Republiky. The place was owned by a husband and wife. The wife was the hostess and t husband cooked in the kitchen. That evening the wife was very sweet and offered us a g table upstairs with a view of the street. Indian food, Mexican food, spicy food in general just starting to really gain favour in Prague then, so the restaurants weren't generally th busy. Beta had never tried Indian food, so I chose something for her. It was curried broccoli, cauliflower and potatoes, served with rice – a dish other girl friends had liked – and chicken curry for myself and I had the hostess bring us fresh nan bread too. When food came, I of course dove straight in, dipping the warm nan bread into the curry sauc and savouring in the chicken with delight. I looked up to gauge Beta's reaction. She hac maybe taken one bite, and was sitting there looking at me with these two large tears in eyes. "Is it too spicy?" She nodded, like a child who has fallen down, surprised and hurt "What do you want?" I asked. "Anything!" "Bramborachky and slivovice," she said. The hostess came and she was very sorry about it. Beta was a good sport as always and she knew I was enjoying my food and let me finish before we left. When I paid I gave the hostess a little something extra and she told us to come back again. It was my fault, I know. Spicy exotic foods were still a novelty in Prague then, and most people were like Beta, a little loath to try anything spicy, preferring the traditional native dishes, which w very mild.

So we ended up back at the Cherna Kochka and had bramborachky and slivovice and w both perfectly happy, and after that went back to my flat and made love. In the morning Beta awoke first, her busy-bright suricata smile would wake me up.

"I'm tired of sleeping, Jamesiku. Entertain me!"

She was easy to entertain, and I liked that. I'd get up most mornings and go down the street to the potraviny and grab a few rohliky and some fruit and cheese. Back at the fla we would have breakfast with coffee or tea.

That morning as we ate, she had a bit of a puzzled expression. When I asked if anything was wrong, Beta said late in the night, after we'd gone to sleep, I had started talking in sleep, that I had held her and, nearly weeping, had said, "Poor Beta! Poor suricate!" Ove and over. We'd had a lot to drink the night before, so I knew that explained it. But Beta troubled – her intuition was working on it. Like I said, I attributed this late night outbur to too much beer, a bit of late night, inebriated lachrymose, if you will. Beta had too mu High Tatry good sense and courtesy to trouble me too much about it. The little stuff she could harp on endlessly, but anything more serious and she would become very quiet, tactful, reserved. In my ignorance then, how little I understood her. Later, someone explained to me that the further east you go in Europe, especially in Ukraine, Slovakia, parts of Russia, the tighter hold women tend to keep on men because of their drinking. Beta's day-to-day harping was something normal in the east, the way girlfriends or wive reigned their partners in, to keep the drinking from getting too destructive.

You think about the night at Ferdinand and how nice Beta had been, so understanding and sympathetic. It was almost as though she'd seen something like that happen before Back in her hometown she was treated as a returning princess whenever she went back sit. She'd managed to escape the small town, the trappings of redneck Slovakia, and e to Prague and was making something of herself. She was doing the same as I was, ng the world, or at least more of it. As with Anna, we were both bound together by the on that we were outsiders, though Beta of course was less so than I, being able to k the language and with home only a few hours' train ride away.

, we were essentially the same, runaways in search of a greater world. Instead of ging us closer together, it actually drove us apart. That was my fault largely. I ished my high destiny very selfishly, it was not something to be shared with anyone. I ight no one else could understand, as though I were the first person to ever venture out the world with dreams of greatness.

a also had a high opinion of herself, and when it ended between us it was my fault. I 't revisit that particular night, or go into what happened. It was part of that destructive , and I will cut to a Sunday morning in spring. The two of us are sitting on a bench ing out at the Vltava and the castle. It is a fine morning, and many people are out. Over the Rudolfinium a movie is being filmed and the whole square is decorated to look like don during the first World War. All the extras are wearing army uniforms and vardian dress.

a and I sit at the bench, both of us looking out at the river, neither of us saying thing. I look over at her and she is quietly sobbing, her lovely suricate smile is gone, igh she bravely fights back the tears. In that moment, I feel sorrier than I have ever felt. a lovely morning and that smile is gone, everything between us is gone and, with that, seems, my whole dream of Prague.

denly, Beta wipes her eyes, looks at me. She reaches over and touches my face. nehow, the smile comes back.

eer up, Jamesey!" she says. "You are looking so depressed!"

get up and go for a walk, passing the movie scene. The action is cut so we make our past the extras, see the director up on the steps of the Rudolfinium barking out orders 1 a megaphone.

's get something to eat," Beta says. But I am not hungry so she goes into a bakery and a blueberry muffin. She breaks off a piece and gives it to me, and we walk, through Town and then, feeling like tourists, across the Charles Bridge and over to Petrin Hill to n the grass. The white blossoms on the trees are really bright in the sun, and young ple are lying in the grass. It seemed then that the spring could save anything, or almost ything.

Waiting for Mr. Novak

The Office of the Czech Government is a handsome, august building on the banks of the Vltava River in what is known as the Straka Academy . Nearby there is a small park whe the Second World War monument sits, and just across the street are the tram stops and Malastranska metro station. From the park you have a nice view of the castle on the hill and on fine afternoons, students sit or lay in the grass reading and talking.

That spring I taught at the government office four days a week, and usually went and re in the grass an hour or two before, or else strolled through the streets of Mala Strana an browsed the Shakespeare and Sons bookshop.

Misha was the secretary to Jan Novak, head of the Office of the Czech government. Her high position notwithstanding, Misha was far from formal; a vivacious, attractive blonde with a sweet, genuine smile. She was in her mid-forties, divorced, with a teenage daught Originally I was sent there to teach her boss, Mr. Novak, but he was usually busy in meetings or away on official state business. So I would teach Misha.

"She needs to practice her English anyway," Mr. Novak said, on one of the rare occasion he spoke to me (his own level of English was excellent, and he passed Cambridge-level exams that year).

Mr. Novak himself was very formal, descended, so I was told, from a very well-to-do old Czech family. He commanded respect with his sedate, impeccable dress and manners. Once he showed me, without ostentatious ceremony, a letter personally signed by Presid Bush, thanking him, Mr. Novak, for his excellent hospitality during the president's recer visit to Prague (this came during the missile shield talks).

As I said I rarely saw Mr. Novak. But he seemed to want me around, for some reason. Instead of just going one day, as was initially planned, Mr. Novak insisted I come four da a week. "He says he is satisfied with you," Misha told me.

But I rarely saw him. I taught Misha and Verona . Verona was Mr. Novak's chief of staff. Both were lovely to teach. Most afternoons we would just sit and chat. They made sure I had plenty of juice or tea and usually there was something sweet – the office was always well-stocked for visitors.

Misha, years before, after the revolution, had worked at Prague Castle for Vaclav Havel. She entertained me with amusing anecdotes from those days, such as when the writer Bohumil Hrabal showed up, in t-shirt and jeans, a bottle of Gambrinus in hand and casually strolled into the Czech president's office shouting "Vashek!" the familiar form of Vaclav. The president would stop whatever he was doing and come out and warmly gree fellow writer. She told me about Havel too, the high-water pants that he preferred n his suits, and of his kindness and humility, and about Mick Jagger, Lou Reed, and host of other celebrated people who came to the castle in those heady, post-Revolution s.

ha knew a lot of people, especially in the arts. She went regularly to concerts, theater mieres and exhibition openings, and to cafes frequented by artists, writers and rnalists, such as the Literary Café near Tyn Church or the Zlate Had (Golden Snake). It s she who recommended places for me to go, writers to read, such as Hrabal and Topol, l tried to interest me in Czech painting and photography, and I enjoyed listening to her .

ona, by contrast, always dressed in black, which matched her black hair and dark, vic eyes. She was born in Slovakia but had lived in Prague many years, was in her early ies, and had a somewhat severe manner. But she had a very warm side too. She just l a strong sense of propriety. She kept a strict watch over the office and especially Mr. 'ak, of whom she thought highly. In fact, she fussed over him so much that, Verona self told me with a laugh; Mr. Novak grew exasperated and shouted, "You are like my ther!"

also true Verona had her moods. They came as suddenly and inexplicably as a summer rm. When these days came, when her wrath was en extent, you could feel a palpable, vy silence in the corridors, and even Misha would speak in whispers. We'd both lower voices, like naughty children, and hide from Verona. Yes, we both nursed a quiet dread Verona , and I think she sensed it and it hurt her feelings, for underneath she was a et, if insecure person. She never showed me these moods, and was always gracious. took a protective liking to me, and enjoyed looking after me in the same way as she did Novak. She kept me stuffed with cookies and chocolates, and once after Christmas she ted me and Misha into her office and served us delicious leftovers from her kitchen le, and we also each drank glasses of white wine and even Verona allowed herself to sh tipsily. We were again like naughty children, only this time Verona too, playing in se high offices while Mr. Novak was away attending to important matters of the State. king back, I think she extended her kindness to me in part because she herself had n a school teacher for many years, and also because she felt embarrassed for me that Novak had relegated his English lessons to his assistants (Not that I minded), and she felt, looking at my scruffy shoes and torn pants, which I'd worn to the pub the night ore, that I needed some looking after.

ce she even read me tarot cards, this after Christmas. Misha was busy that day, and y solemnly Verona brought out the cards and spread them out. After reading them, she ked at me with some relief. "I thought I was going to have to give you bad news," she d. But as it turned out, everything was going to be all right for me, providing I just took ter care of myself and ate better.

vards Misha, Verona was also like a mother, feeling, I think, that it was high time Misha ınd someone" and remarried. I think she even tried a bit of match-making with us, sha and I, for she would pat and play with Misha's hair and say Misha was beautiful and e me confirm it. Misha and I would exchange a wink. Other days Verona would be spicuously absent, leaving us alone together. This was a great relief to Misha and I and would relax in her office looking at videos on her computer. She would show me clips of ssive Attack, Tom Waits, Nick Cave and other groups she liked, and we discussed people l places and gossip.

y we never went out anywhere together, I don't know. We were always making plans; to e a beer up at Letna Park in the spring, or she'd take me to Zlate Had or a concert, but whatever reason, we never did. As the spring gave way to a bright, rich summer we still ked of going places, and even with the arrival of a brown-gold autumn.

t all of this was a very small part of our relations, something felt occasionally rather n discussed, and for the most part we just enjoyed relaxed, un-serious afternoons together. Often there was business – Mr. Novak was always dropping last-minute, urgen business into her lap, from correspondence, to flight confirmations to his dry cleaning – many times I would arrive and Misha would apologize and just sign the attendance form and we'd say, '*Pristye*!" meaning "Next time!" Other days, if the afternoon was fine and I was enjoying my reading in the Kampa, or feeling lazy and sitting in a café, I'd send a te to Misha saying I was busy and that was OK too.

For such a small country, there was a lot of important business in the Czech Republic tl year. There was the controversial plan by the Bush Administration to build an anti-miss defense shield near a town called Pribrem; also Klaus was up for re-election that year an of course there was the Czechs' turn at the EU presidency. Just after they assumed it, tl Russians threatened to cut off gas supplies to Europe over a long-standing dispute with Ukraine over rates. The gas line ran through Ukraine . It was Mr. Novak, who with his boss, then-Prime Minister Topolanek who flew to Moscow and helped mediate a late-nigl agreement that kept the gas flowing.

Actually one of my few memories of Mr. Novak came following that Moscow trip. Every n and again, with a sort of remorse, he would be in the office and would send word to Misl that he wanted to see me.

That afternoon Misha came into the little kitchen excited. "Mr. Novak wants to see you today. He is waiting!" I grabbed my bag and followed Misa. She escorted me into the offic and then ran back out to bring us refreshments.

Mr. Novak's office was large and impressive, with generous views of the Vltava and Pragu skyline. The furniture (the office had just been renovated that year) was elegant, antique preserved from the days of the First Republic .

On that day Mr. Novak had just returned from his trip to Moscow . His youngish face (he was only about thirty) was tired and worn beneath his expensive haircut, and the sleeve his immaculate, monogrammed shirt were rolled up. There was a stack of paperwork awaiting his attention that had been brought in by both Misha and Verona . Since he wa often out of town, the days he was in town were catch up days, and often I would see visitors who had some business with him line up outside in Misha's office. But evidently didn't want to get right into the paperwork that afternoon and wanted a few minutes to chat. He would work late into the night (he preferred the late hours for working, which meant Misha would have to stay late too).

I was always self-conscious and embarrassed on these rare meetings, aware of my beat u shoes and wrinkled clothing in contrast to Mr. Novak's impeccable dress, and also aware that I was keeping him from his duties.

That afternoon we talked about his trip. Mr. Novak, perhaps because he knew I'd been a journalist in the States and in fact still was one on the side, was always reticent on offici matters, but also just because he was generally reserved, though always courteous, to those of lower rank.

I asked about meeting Putin, and he nodded, rubbing the purple bags under his eyes.

"We went out to his estate," Mr. Novak said.

I was very curious to get his impressions of Putin, but seeing my enthusiasm, he waved off with a tired, indulgent ghost of a smile.

"It was nothing," he said. "We shook hands." He made a couple other short, dry remarks and I could see it was no use pursuing the matter any further. That was disappointing because I'd been following the news reports keenly and was anxious to get his point of vi But of course it would have been inappropriate for me to press too hard.

We chatted a few minutes longer, and then, uncrossing his legs and clasping his hands together, Mr. Novak announced he had to get back to work. As always, when we rose he was very courteous and we shook hands earnestly, and he smiled a little deprecatingly fc all the other lost lessons and assured me we would meet again soon and regularly. "I nee to practice my tenses," he said.

"—and phrasal verbs," I reminded him.

, precisely."

xchanged a serious nod as always, and then I went back out to reception. Misha was at work at her computer. But she looked up and smiled, happy I'd had a chance to get nd see Mr. Novak for a change. I told her how Mr. Novak and I had got on well and had nised each other to pursue the lessons with renewed vigor.

nis Misha and I exchanged a conspiratorial wink.

you tomorrow, James," she said, flashing her sweet, genuine smile as always.

The New Europe

I had lessons with Tomas at the Straka Academy on Friday mornings. He was in his lat twenties, clean-shaven and with an energetic, engaging personality. He'd spent a year ir America a few years before, so he'd developed a near-native level of English. He manage pass his proficiency exam with only minimal assistance from me, but we enjoyed each others' company, and he knew I needed the money, so he kept up the lessons even after really didn't need them.

Most of the people in the Office of the Government that year were preparing to pass the English and French proficiency tests because the Czechs were to assume the EU presidency the following spring. There was a busy, hectic air of preparation all that year and those of us teaching there had plenty of work.

Friday mornings generally weren't too bad, unless some last-minute business came up. Tomas was working, if I remember correctly, for Alexander Vondra, a former ambassado the United States who at that time was Minister of EU Affairs. That year was also the ye of the U.S. elections and we spent many lessons discussing Hilary versus Obama follow the primaries.

We also enjoyed discussing Czech politics, and Tomas was able to provide lots of first-h knowledge of this or that MP or other high-ranking official. Klaus, for instance, we dubb "Kashparek," which means joker in Czech. Tomas told me this was the name the Czech president was known by in Brussels , for his foot-stamping, vitriolic anti-EU outbursts. "It's like he wants to be a dissident," Tomas remarked. "I think he envies Havel for his international stature and reputation as a dissident. But Havel did it back during Communism, when it was dangerous. Havel went to prison for it, where Klaus and his k were too afraid, too conservative. And now, when it's safe, and he is president, it's like h wants to be a dissident. He craves the reputation, the acclaim of Havel . He's an egoist."

On many days I brought in books, and we'd either sit in the big room on the first floor usually reserved for press conferences (we'd take turns in the prime minister's seat). I brought in books – Graham Greene's The Third Man, Truman Capote's Handcarved Coff Hemingway's The Sun Also Rises, and we'd take turns reading and sometimes even play the parts. It was an entertaining way to blow off an hour.

Like Misha and Verona , Tomas had weeks when he was busy, and he also would send text message in advance and the next lesson just sign it off. I didn't mind when he cancelled, since it left me with a free Friday morning. I'd go and grab a late breakfast at Bohemia Bagel or the Globe and sit and read until I had to go back to the Straka Acade at three for my lesson with Misha and Verona .

It's tempting for me to feel guilty, to say, look the Czech taxpayers aren't paying their elected officials and bureaucrats to sit around and read Hemingway or gossip about the ident. But in truth I think it benefited both of us enormously. On my end, I got to 1 a lot about the so-called New Europe, which before the crisis came was in full bloom, it allowed Tomas to practice his English in a relaxed, entertaining way and take a k from his work. The euro zone was strong then, and although efforts to get a stitution approved were slow and frustrating, there was a feeling of excitement, a sort of aucratic zeal, in helping shape this new idea. I mean, that's the feeling you got when spoke to people like Tomas, and Daniel and others.

e for example Tomas' report, "A Return to Europe ." He brought this into a lesson one ning. He'd been tasked by his boss to write the report as part of a conference that the ity director was going to attend, I believe.

as a fluent, articulate, very readable report. It detailed modern Czech history, from the s of the First Republic , through the Second World War and Communism and through twenty years of post-Communism. Essentially, Tomas' felt that for the Czech's the oming EU presidency was the culmination of long and tough process of gearing Czech cy and thinking back to its historical home, Europe, after a half century of being a et satellite.

say, it was an interesting report, and we had a good discussion about it afterwards, you could see from the report that not only Tomas, but many at Straka Academy , had hopes of the Czechs playing a key role in the New Europe. That's why they made fun of is, the famous Euroskeptic. Like the time Klaus left ODS, the party he himself had ided, after the party voted in support of Topolanek over Prague Mayor Pavel Bem, who is had urged the party to back as new party head. The whole controversy started with is feeling that Topolanek, then the prime minister, was too EU friendly. After the party d in support of Topolanek, not only did Klaus leave the party, but he erased party nbers names from his mobile phone.

don't need people like Klaus in the New Europe." Tomas felt this rather than said it ctly. I mean, like most, he respected Klaus's work as an economist, and his role in ing reconstruct the Czech economy following the collapse of communism. But now it ned the president had become a vain stick in the mud, determined to the spotlight on Czech Republic, and on himself, rather than have it shift to Brussels. Of course, sidering the course of Czech history, when so often a foreign body dictated policy, one st admit Klaus's reluctance is understandable, if not sound. And the crisis that hit ope a couple years later, following the bankruptcy in Greece, Klaus's hard-line position vindicated to a degree.

in those days, in government circles at least not in the street, where most people had dly a clue what the EU actually did, there was a certain buzz: the time has come, to do t Napolean, what Hitler, the Communists, had failed to do: create a truly strong and ted Europe at last.

nember though that we weren't zealots or ideologues, just two guys passing the time in English lesson. But as I said, I know for me it was very beneficial, and on Tomas' end, I ik it was beneficial too. Not only did he practice his English, but I would like to think I ed him blow off a bit of steam (he really did work a lot), and also to think about his k in a relaxed environment.

got to be close enough that when he got married, on a cold morning in early spring, he ted me. The ceremony was held in the big church just off Andel Plaza . There were ny weddings scheduled that morning, in and out like an assembly line. I recognized ers from the Straka Academy who had also been invited, and afterward we all had shots *livovice.*

Vratya at Shakespeare and Sons

Just off Donksa Street, Krymska runs from the of the hill gently down a cracked, cobble lane to a small park at the bottom. Along the way, there is the Barracuda, which serves Mexican food that was very bad and over-priced but that gradually improved over time. interior was all decked out in its Mexican theme, and when you placed your order the waiter called the cook downstairs on his mobile and in a few minutes the order came up a small lift.

Downhill from the Barracuda is Shakespeare and Sons. Now the hours are on the door, the place never opened at a set time. If there had been a lively, long party the night befo then it would open very late in the afternoon. The owner, David, wore spectacles and sometimes a beard, and he was reserved and soft-spoken. Sometimes he was there, and other days he was at the main branch in Mala Strana. Other days there was Kristina, a wispy, pretty young brunette who reminded me of Amelie, maybe because she often play the soundtrack for the movie and if it wasn't busy, listened to the music with dreamy Amelie-like eyes.

There were two or three others who worked there, and anyway, one of them would be th when it opened, and they would mop the floors with the chairs still on top of the tables, with the front door opened to let in fresh air and drive out stale cigarette smoke from th night before.

Usually when I saw them cleaning I would take a walk around the block, down the stree and around to Sebastopol and up to Donska and back down the hill. If I took my time usually the bar would be open for business by then. Inside there were English newspape and the Economist, and nobody minded if you picked one and sat down and read it with paying for it. I'd order a tea or a Coke with lime or a mug of Bernard, depending on what had to do, and then sat and read the International Herald Tribune or the Guardian. The was always lots of news on the war and later on, the crisis and Obama.

Vratislav Brbinec came in early. His flat was just down the street. Vratya, as everybody called him, was a saxophonist in the Plastic People of the Universe, the legendary Czech underground group from Communist times. He and other members of the group were arrested and sent to prison during the 1970s for staging a concert without approval fron the authorities. These days, the surviving members of the group, including Vratya, still played often around Prague , in places like Lucerna Bar, and even toured internationally occasionally.

Now in his sixties, Vratya was lean, almost gaunt, with long, stringy grey hair and shrew cat-like eyes which crouched behind a pair of black-rimmed, owl-like glasses. Vratya mo slowly, his shoulders stooped, and he spoke English and Czech in the same, slow gravel baritone.

was always dressed in the same clothes, or similar clothes: a brown corduroy jacket, k trousers and, if the weather was nice, a pair of sandals, which exposed raw, thorny nails. He could have passed easily for an aging poet or literature professor or, as he was, zz musician.

sunny afternoons, he enjoyed drinking wine, on other days something stronger. I saw at the café often but for a long time didn't try to speak to him. Often people came and ed him, and listening to their conversations, the ones in English, he struck me as culate and interesting, urbane. I picked up bits and pieces of his story from others. r the revolution he had imigrated to Canada and spent many years there, and had a and daughter. But he had come back to Prague and had a girlfriend here and, as I l, the Plastic People still performed regularly.

ne time around then there was a story in the New York Times, I think, and in the story a n was quoted as saying that he thought the surviving members of Plastic People drank nuch and were "dirty." I put this in just to show that there were different opinions. true Vratya drank a lot, but then most of us did. There were nights when he would stay lly late and be unable to walk home, and the barman or someone would have to assist the short way down the hill to his flat.

loved jazz – Duke Ellington, John Coltrane, Miles Davis, and so on. Often the bar staff uld obligingly throw on something to his taste as he sat over his drink. "In My Solitude," Sophisticated Lady." He loved these songs, and when the music started, came floating r the smoky tables of the bar, Vratya would slip into a nodding trance, his gaunt, skered face lighting up with ecstasy.

I said, I didn't try to speak to him for a long time. Partly because I was shy and didn't nt to bother him, but also because I generally didn't talk to anyone at Shakespeare's. I oyed reading or writing, having a drink and enjoying the warm, books-and-music nosphere and looking at the people. Or if Kristina was working, I liked watching her ely figure drift back and forth at the bar, or to watch her face as she stared at something her laptop. But still, it was a comfort to have Vratya there; to me he was a kind of living nument to the country's turbulent past. That comment may come off as obvious or even ronizing to some, but it's how I felt for what it's worth.

ner interesting and celebrated people came in from time to time: artists, writers, rnalists, musicians. It wasn't unusual to see someone being interviewed, or otographed. But low key was the unspoken code, so you pretended not to notice it and nt on with your reading. It's true the crowd at times could be a bit effete, stand-offish, at st compared to the easy brotherhood of the Zaba, but then you didn't notice that either. er all, the benefits of Shakespeare and Sons far outweighed any downsides.

expats, there was a wonderful room in back stocked to the ceiling with books in glish. There were books in Czech, really old ones, in front in the café but they were really t decoration. Nobody minded if, on a cold day, or if you were just broke, you went in and in back for hours reading a book you could not afford to buy and just ordered one nk. Also, if you were broke, David would always by any used books you had, he paid enty five percent I think, so you could always scrape together a few crowns if you were lly desperate.

course, you tried to make up for all this generosity later when you got paid, you made a nt of buying a book, and even ordered something to eat. Also for a long time there was a at-up old Apple computer in the back where you could check e-mail or browse the ernet for free. David eventually got rid of the computer, I think in part to discourage riff f who were starting to abuse it, but also because he wanted to expand the café.

e café was also a decent place to write or study; most afternoons and evenings the tables re lit up with laptops. It was Hemingway who said you had cafes where you met people d other cafes where you worked or read. I didn't write very often at Shakespeare's – I nd I wrote best at Bohemia Bagel or the Globe and I preferred to write in the morning. akespeare's was my reading and people watching café.

The day I finally met Vratya was when Obama came to Prague. Obama's visit was very much talked about in the press and among my students, and it was one of my students who gave me a special invite to hear the speech up close in the VIP section. Anyway, aft the speech I raced back to Vrsovice and into Shakespeare's. It was a warm spring day ar the café had just opened. Vratya was sitting at the bar having a drink with the girlfriend the barman who was working that day.

I was full of excitement, the buzz of the crowds. This was during Obama's first days as president and Obamamania had swept Europe too. I began babbling about the speech, r impressions, to the barman and his girl, who I knew, and anyone else who would listen. They did listen, intently, for they were curious too, and it was then I noticed Vratya was listening too and his eyes were lit up and keen, and he even had a bit of a grin. He asked couple of questions and soon we fell into conversation.

It was like we both had been waiting for just such an opportunity. He suggested we get a table and then we ordered beer. The barman put on some jazz and we talked about it, I think he played some Miles Davis that day, and drank beer and ended up talking for several hours. He listened to me rattle on about the Obama visit with interest and some amusement.

"You are very optimistic," he said.

We talked about the days of the Prague Spring, which the president had brought up in h speech.

"Yes, we were very optimistic then too," he said. "But then it turned out to be a false optimism."

He talked a bit about the time he spent in prison, or I asked about it, I think.

"Why were you in prison?"

He laughed. "For being a jazz musician."

After that I sat with Vratya regularly. His moods shifted. Sometimes he was already drun when I arrived, and he could be ebullient and talkative or surly and morose, distant.

"I am an old man," he would sometimes say, miserably.

And you could tell it hurt him if he saw your attention wavering, or if you avoided him when you came in. Sometimes you did, but you felt sorry for it afterward and you were happy when he news to share: the group was going to Tel Aviv for a concert.

Then he would be gone for a few days, and when he returned, he was restored, energized well-known, traveling musician again with the world very much with him. You were happ for him and asked many questions about Tel Aviv and be interested in him all over again He saw through this and though he still remembered the other times he was modest and overlooked it and invited you to sit down for a drink.

He knew a great many people, and a great many people knew him, yet he was very often alone, alone with the old age and melancholy, the loneliness that was coming as sure an soft as the crooning of a Lester Young solo, a solo full of Young's sweet melancholy and nostalgia but that left no euphoria as a chaser, but rather only the empty beginning of a hangover.

But that was on the bad days; he had many good days too, days when the people came a sat and talked and there were reminisces and plans for another concert and you could se the rush of life seize him like a brisk wind and his cat-like eyes lost their glazed, melancholy look and were animated and sharp again.

Vratya noticed me going through my own bouts of drinking and depression then – I think he sensed they were the reason why I sometimes avoided him, and he knew that and he forgave me for it. "Kam des, curak!" he would tease, or half-tease.

One afternoon I invited him to the Zaba. We had already had a few so we walked slowly u the hill. Kuba and Lenka and a few other people were already there having drinks up at t bar. Vratya wanted to sit in the back room so we all went and sat with him. I introduced him to everyone, and I think Vratya could tell I was kind of showing him off. He was fortable there, as most people are at the Zaba, but he was both flattered and arrassed by the attention (as if I needed to introduce him to his own countrymen). already been drinking and soon he began fading. Before that I noticed him regarding n the booth with his owl eyes. I think he had been observing me for some time, while I ed with Kuba and the others.

want to belong here, to be like everyone," he said, curiously echoing what Kuba had . "But you must go your own way. You must take care about yourself."

that he rose to pay.

that I still saw him often at Shakespeare and Sons, and we still sat together and k and talked. Other days he would have company, and still other days one or both of ould want to be left alone. When the time came for me to leave Prague – I was bound stanbul – I talked about it a bit with Vratya, and I think he was happy for me. I don't v what he really thought: perhaps he was glad to finally have me out of his hair, or 't care one way or the other. But he seemed happy; I think we both knew it was high I was headed somewhere.

or Vratya, he was already home, and I imagine right now, if he's not on tour, he's ably at Shakespeare, having a drink. It will still be winter there too. He is listening to music, or perhaps his solitude, and waiting for the spring to come.

then we were always waiting for spring in Prague.

ngtime in Prague is an exciting time and the time for seeing people and making plans. beer gardens at Riegrovy Sady and Letna open up and are full every evening. At the gardens you see all the people you haven't seen all winter and they seem to have been rnating and now they suddenly appear again alive and well and it is a joy to see them, resh and new as the spring.

long picnic tables are full and if a match is playing on the big TV screens. The osphere is loud and and the beer lines are long. But you don't mind because it's spring, you don't even mind that the price of beer has gone up again. The guys pumping out glasses of Gambrinus by the dozen usually remember you. They greet you and it's just last summer was only yesterday and the whole long winter had never existed.

re were always the Nick and Joanne, and Dave and Orla and the many others from the don Institute. Dave and Nick passed joints mixed with tobacco and we talked and k beer and enjoyed the fresh air and sunshine sitting under a canopy of trees that quickly gathering new leaves again, and would explode in a matter of weeks. Then e was Rueben and Larkin and even Terry came, looking a little pale and anxious away the neon-blue gaze of the nightclubs, where I was used to seeing him. Larkin, the an, was always good to have around, especially for the football matches. Except over he became a little too comfortable with Czech life, a little too "Czech," as some of our ch friends observed. In those days if a man was taken short, no one looked down on if he found a bush and relieved himself behind it. But Larkin would stand up in the garden, walk to the back fence, drop his shorts and do it right there with his back to crowds.

he people came from around the city – Americans, Brits, French, Germans, Aussies, sians and of course Czechs – and with the slowly lengthening days there was a feeling life was opening up and you became excited, knowing the the evenings would get ger and there were many more nights to come.

danger was always in getting too excited, too impatient and finally, too drunk. Then e would be scenes that could spoil the evening, such as when people began arguing ut the war or politics. Nick and I especially had to be careful. He was from Liverpool, pectacled, with a large birthmark on his face and, like me, could be troublesome and e when he drank too much. But for the most part there were only the good evenings good people and the beer garden and the spring.

Then there was the Kampa. It was Guillaume and Chloe who showed me the Kampa. They were students from France who that first spring were studying in Prague. Since I w new to the city too and it was my first spring we enjoyed discovering the city together ar showing each other places. They showed me the Kampa, I showed them Riegrovy Sady. We would go to the Kampa on fine evenings and spread a blanket out on the grass near river with their other friends. We would pass around bottles of wine and talk about Prag and literature and music. Guillaume had big frizzy hair and glasses and was very funny Chloe was dark and petite and lovely, she sat in the grass barefoot in her flower dresses and she had a soft, pleasant voice and liked to give you little presents. All of the student shared a big flat in Letna near the Sparta football stadium and they invited me over for dinner and wine, and we sat on the floor upstairs and listened to music on Chloe's CD player. I remember liking the music and Chloe burned me a copy that evening and gave to me before I left.

They were all young, and always liked to go roaming and wandering through Prague's streets at night. Sometimes I went with them and sometimes I lost them – too much win but the evenings were always lovely.

Sitting in the beer garden, or walking over a bridge and looking out at the Vltava, you always made a promise to the city and with the spring, especially after that first winter. You made a promise to do things differently, to drink less, to be healthy, find ways enjoy and prolong the spring, to do better work and to grow.

Later, that vow was forgotten and vanished, just as quickly as the spring, and you could never remember it. Sometime in deep summer, when it was hot and you felt bored and ready for autumn, you tried to remember what it was you had promised – some years yo even forgot to even do that much – but you could not remember and then the winter wo come again and you would never remember it until it was spring again.

But in the end that's what we came to love about our city, Prague. The spring never faile to come and when it did you were just as excited – no, more excited – than you were in t years past because this time you would not forget all the things you promised. The prom of spring could just be false optimism, as that 1968 spring was, when Soviet tanks rolle into the city and crushed the hopes of people like Vratislav Brbinec, or when our own destructive impulses got in the way. But we didn't think so. Prague always delivered, eve if we didn't. That's why, like Vratya, we still waited for the spring to come.

www.ingramcontent.com/pod-product-compliance
Ingram Content Group UK Ltd.
Pitfield, Milton Keynes, MK11 3LW, UK
UKHW041834200726
13854UKWH00003BA/1132